Samuel French Acting Edition

Project Murder – The Elimination Challenge
or
Murder on the Runway

I0591908

by Don Zolidis

SAMUEL FRENCH

SAMUELFRENCH.COM   SAMUELFRENCH.CO.UK

FOR PRODUCTION ENQUIRIES

UNITED STATES AND CANADA
Info@SamuelFrench.com
1-866-598-8449

UNITED KINGDOM AND EUROPE
Plays@SamuelFrench.co.uk
020-7255-4302

Each title is subject to availability from Samuel French, depending upon country of performance. Please be aware that *PROJECT MURDER – THE ELIMINATION CHALLENGE OR MURDER ON THE RUNWAY* may not be licensed by Samuel French in your territory. Professional and amateur producers should contact the nearest Samuel French office or licensing partner to verify availability.

MUSIC USE NOTE

Licensees are solely responsible for obtaining formal written permission from copyright owners to use copyrighted music in the performance of this play and are strongly cautioned to do so. If no such permission is obtained by the licensee, then the licensee must use only original music that the licensee owns and controls. Licensees are solely responsible and liable for all music clearances and shall indemnify the copyright owners of the play(s) and their licensing agent, Samuel French, against any costs, expenses, losses and liabilities arising from the use of music by licensees. Please contact the appropriate music licensing authority in your territory for the rights to any incidental music.

IMPORTANT BILLING AND CREDIT REQUIREMENTS

If you have obtained performance rights to this title, please refer to your licensing agreement for important billing and credit requirements.

PRODUCTION HISTORY

Anoka High School, Anoka, Minnesota: September 21-23, 2016
Trinity Catholic High School, Fort Smith, Arizona: November 21, 2016
Greenville High School, Greenville, Texas: December 9-10, 2016
Borah High School, Boise, Idaho: December 1-31, 2016
Twin Rivers High School, Sacramento, California: March 1-31, 2017

CHARACTERS

THE DETECTIVE

CAROL-ANN PERKINS – Female, middle-aged, a total mess, clumsy, but intense.

THE CONTESTANTS

ANNIE – Female, good-natured, daffy, a little bit older, fifties-to-sixties.

SHIVA – Female, goth, vicious, terrifying, twenties-to-thirties.

PRESIDENT GENERAL POPE JOHNSON – Male, fabulous, probably wears amazing glasses, might wear shoes that have wheels in them and roll around the stage, twenties-to-thirties.

IFEZ – Male, from an indeterminate foreign country, does his own thing, might wear a boa or heels, probably has exotic facial hair, twenties-to-forties.

LUKE – Male, sweet, kind of dumb, good-looking, twenties.

In my mind, President is African American and Ifez is Hispanic, but any of the roles may be played by an actor of any race or ethnicity. All other roles may be played by one male and one female actor. Most of the roles below are gender-neutral, meaning that they can be played as either male or female – there is absolutely no need for a male actor to be required to make all of the characters male, for example. (In the case of Becky and Vanessa, the characters should be played as female). It should be obvious to the audience that the same two actors are playing every part, so no need for elaborate costumes. Part of the humor of the show comes from the fact that these changes are so outlandish and obvious. You may also decide to cast separate actors in each role to create a larger cast.

CHIEF BAILIHEW – Police chief.

DETECTIVE MOSLEY – Probably female, a high-ranking officer.

OFFICER JONES – A police officer (played by the actor playing Chief).

OFFICER NIGELA – A police officer (played by the actor playing Mosley).

ALIANA – A supermodel, host of the show (played by the actor playing Mosley).

TOSCA – Elegant, immaculately-coiffed advisor to the contestants (played by the actor playing Chief).

PIETER – Norwegian fashion designer, judge (played by the actor playing Chief).

SAMANTHA – Editor-in-chief of a fashion magazine, judge (played by the actor playing Mosley).

BLAIZE – Fashion reporter on E TV (played by the actor playing Chief).

UMA – Fashion reporter on E TV (played by the actor playing Mosley).

BECKY – An ordinary woman model (played by the actor playing Mosley).

VANESSA – An ordinary woman model (played by the actor playing Chief).

AUTHOR'S NOTES

Alternate Endings: There is one standard ending and six possible alternate endings for this show. At intermission, the audience should be given a ballot listing all six contestants (Carol-Ann, Annie, Shiva, President, Ifez, Luke) as possible killers. Your production may decide to use the ending voted on by the audience, or choose a different one if you wish.

Costume Pieces: These should all be pre-made to make things easier on the actors. Feel free to make this as ridiculous as possible.

Brackets & Cutting: Some of the jokes in the play may be inappropriate for your community. Dialogue in [brackets] may be cut, and I have suggested alternate jokes and dialogue where applicable.

ACT ONE

*(Lights up on the police commandant's desk. **BAILIHEW** is sitting with his hand on the phone. **DETECTIVE MOSLEY** is standing nearby.)*

BAILIHEW. We got this today. Ready?

MOSLEY. Sure.

BAILIHEW. You sure you're ready?

MOSLEY. Yes!

*(Lights up slightly on a **PERSON IN SHADOW** elsewhere on stage. If possible, they use an auto-tune or something similar to disguise their voice.)*

PERSON IN SHADOW. New York Police Department, this is a friendly heads-up. I hope you've been tuning into Project Design, airing on Bravo network Wednesdays at nine p.m. Eastern Time.

MOSLEY. What –?

BAILIHEW. Shhh!

PERSON IN SHADOW. Sponsored by Ulta, Sephora, and Marie Claire magazine. It's a great show. Really fun to watch. And it's going to be even more fun when I kill one of the contestants on live television. Ha ha ha ha.

MOSLEY. Wow.

BAILIHEW. Shh! There's more.

PERSON IN SHADOW. Ha ha ha ha ha. Ha ha ha ha.

(Short pause.)

Ha ha ha ha.

(Short pause.)

PERSON IN SHADOW. That's it. I'm killing someone on live television. Peace out.

(Lights out on **PERSON IN SHADOW.***)*

BAILIHEW. Thoughts?

MOSLEY. I don't think you can do a peace out after a death threat. It's so wrong. It violates the entire purpose of the peace out.

BAILIHEW. No what do you think we should do about the death threat?!

MOSLEY. We tune in on Wednesday. It sounds really exciting.

BAILIHEW. You want us to *tune in*?

MOSLEY. Why are you asking me?! You always do this, you have the answer in your own mind, and then you ask me and you *expect* me to come up with the same answer! This is why I have stress headaches, sir.

BAILIHEW. Mosley!

MOSLEY. Sorry sir. I'm having trouble at home. My cat, he's... he's unhappy. He's not using the litter box properly. My life is a nightmare.

BAILIHEW. I'm sorry to hear that.

MOSLEY. We'll get through it. I just need a lot of prayers right now. And Febreze.

BAILIHEW. All right, look. We've got to get somebody on this – Now I think that –

*(***CAROL-ANN** *enters.)*

CAROL-ANN. Knock knock! Hello.

BAILIHEW. Officer Perkins, I don't believe I called you in here.

CAROL-ANN. That's okay. Because I sensed danger and I am alert. You want to see my preparedness stance? It's like this.

(She does her preparedness stance.)

BAILIHEW. Were you listening at the door again?

CAROL-ANN. When you're as finely-tuned as I am, you just feel it. Like the Force.

BAILIHEW. So that's a yes?

CAROL-ANN. Yes sir. At the door.

MOSLEY. Perkins –

CAROL-ANN. Call me Carol-Ann.

MOSLEY. Perkins, if you don't mind, we have some very serious business to attend to. And some bonding.

BAILIHEW. There won't be any bonding.

MOSLEY. He says that, but there will probably be bonding.

BAILIHEW. Nope.

MOSLEY. So if you could just wait outside please?

CAROL-ANN. I get it. I got you. It's a guy thing. Like in the restroom.

BAILIHEW. There's nothing going on in the restroom.*

CAROL-ANN. The sauna. No one's wearing any clothes. It's sweaty –*

> (*These two lines may be cut.)

BAILIHEW. Do you mind?

CAROL-ANN. I'll just be outside using my imagination then.

> (*She backs out, knocks something over.*)

Whoops. Little stumble. Normally I'm like a cat.

> (*She makes a cat motion, knocks something else over.*)

> (*She's out.*)

BAILIHEW. All right, I want to get our best man on this –

MOSLEY. That's going to be Harwick –

BAILIHEW. I thought the same thing.

> (**CAROL-ANN** *is back.*)

CAROL-ANN. Yo um... I couldn't help but listening in again – you said "best man on this" – and with all due respect, your best man ain't a man. Boom.

> (*She stands there.*)

BAILIHEW. You know what, we do have a job for you. The vice-presidential motorcade needs a few good cops to accompany him –

CAROL-ANN. What? That dirtbag?

MOSLEY. This is the vice president you're talking about –

CAROL-ANN. Not doing it. I'm not into politics. So here's what happens: We go full Miss Congeniality up on this thang. I go undercover –

BAILIHEW. No –

CAROL-ANN. I develop a persona – I'm a designer, I'm eccentric, yet sensual – you can't figure me out. Where did she come from? How does she have these skills? My use of color is phenomenal –

BAILIHEW. Are you listening?

CAROL-ANN. A good cop never listens to the wrong people. So then – I dominate the competition – it's stunning, I win the whole thing – they try to kill me, that's when I strike.

MOSLEY. This is completely unrealistic.

CAROL-ANN. I fill the Sandra Bullock role. I'm amazing. And...here's the kicker... I fall for one of the other designers...romantically.

BAILIHEW. This is actually a real issue, Perkins, you can't –

CAROL-ANN. Oh sure we'll fight it at first. I'll have a bad feeling about it. But I won't be able to contain myself any longer. There's longing. There's fire in our loins. A late night session. [He or she looks over at me, I'm not picky –]*
– Lets go of the fabric in the Singer sewing machine – The fabric tumbles to the ground as we make out like animals. Hands and feet going everywhere. Kama Sutra stuff. And you know what? My lover is the killer. Shocking. No one saw it coming. Boom. Case solved. Murder averted. I get a spread in Marie Claire

---

*This line may be changed to "He looks over at me."

magazine and ten thousand dollars in prize money from an internet fashion company.

> *(Pause.)*

You're considering it.

BAILIHEW. No we're not.

MOSLEY. The vice-presidential motorcade –

CAROL-ANN. He can wait in traffic like the rest of the scum!

BAILIHEW. Perkins, we need a competent detective on this. Go home. Get psychiatric help. You're not getting this job.

CAROL-ANN. Oh. Aw gee. I do this all the time! I get excited about seeing myself in a Sandra Bullock role. I don't even look good in a bikini. No one wants to see that. That's probably why I'm alone. You know. Without love. That probably explains it. I'll go home now. Get one of those frozen pizzas. Eat the whole thing. Cry during it. I probably deserve this life.

BAILIHEW. Okay.

CAROL-ANN. I'll probably be so sad that I'll call the commissioner and tell him everything I know about the Jenkins case, and how that money that was supposed to be evidence disappeared and how I had no idea who did that, even though you were suddenly able to get that new truck – and I'll be crying while I email him the photos I took of you with the cash.

BAILIHEW. I'm sorry?

CAROL-ANN. What?

BAILIHEW. Are you threatening me?

CAROL-ANN. Do I sound like I'm threatening you? That would be crazy. Like a fox.

BAILIHEW. Um...can I talk to you in private?

CAROL-ANN. Nope. Give me the job. Undercover.

BAILIHEW. I'll have to arrange it with the producers –

CAROL-ANN. Do it.

> *(Lights change.)*

(Theme music for Project Design.*)

VOICE OF ALIANA. We took twelve of the greatest and up-and-coming fashion designers and set them a simple task. Succeed or die. The finalists will have their clothes featured in New York's fashion week, which is awesome. It really is. The winning designer will have their pieces in Marie Claire magazine and many other places on the internet! Ten thousand dollars to start your own private studio, a series of customized tattoos, and free representation by Creative Artists Agency, who will represent you if you end up in prison.

Because in the world of fashion, you either make the cut. Or you get cut.

Project Design!

> *(Lights on **SHIVA**, elsewhere on the stage, mugging for the camera.)*

Our remaining designers!

Shiva!

SHIVA. I didn't come here to play. I came here to slay. You might not like me, but then again, I might not care. Ooh.

> *(She poses and lights switch.)*

VOICE OF ALIANA. Ifez!

> *(Lights on **IFEZ**.)*

IFEZ. I am Ifez. So I just talk into the camera then? Are we recording this? We're recording this part? Why didn't someone tell me we were starting?

VOICE OF ALIANA. Luke!

> *(Lights on **LUKE**.)*

LUKE. I design clothes for beautiful people. To make them more beautiful. Like me. Look at me. Go ahead. If you dare.

---

*Licensees should create an original composition or use a song in the Public Domain.

(He poses and lights switch.)

VOICE OF ALIANA. President!

*(Lights on **PRESIDENT**.)*

PRESIDENT. My name is President. I'm from the future, y'all. And I'm here to take you with me.

(He stares forward.)

...I'm not saying anything else. You can keep the camera on me, I'm not saying anything more.

(He stares forward.)

You can move the lights now. Go ahead. Fine. I'll just keep staring.

(He stares forward.)

You love me, audience. You are falling in love with –

(Lights switch.)

VOICE OF ALIANA. Annie!

*(Lights up on **ANNIE**.)*

ANNIE. Hi. I'm Annie. I just love being here. I'm a single mom chasing her dream, and it is such an honor to be here in New York with these amazing people. Pose. Oh I'm supposed to pose?

(She tries to pose.)

VOICE OF ALIANA. Project Design!

(Lights up on the Project Design runway.)

*(**ALIANA**, a former supermodel, is standing next to **TOSCA**, an elegantly dressed person.)*

ALIANA. Designers. Welcome to week six of the ten-week competition. Only five of you remain. Once again we are sorry that Geraldine attacked so many of you last week. We will have safe rooms available if there is to be more crying.

*(**IFEZ** raises his hand.)*

I'm not taking questions right now Ifez.

IFEZ. I'm not sure I can promise that I won't be crying. I am having issues.

TOSCA. And we will address your concerns. But this wouldn't be Project Design without surprises!

LUKE. Ooh!

ALIANA. Shiva, can you please not glare directly at me?

SHIVA. I am not.

ALIANA. Okay. I'm feeling glares though.

SHIVA. I am merely looking at you.

ALIANA. In an angry way.

IFEZ. It's her normal look.

ALIANA. Very well! Are you prepared for the surprise?!

LUKE. YES!

PRESIDENT. Does it matter if I'm prepared or not, you're still going to do it, right?

ANNIE. This is exciting!

TOSCA. Designers...we have a new competitor joining us today.

(Big reaction from the contestants.)

ANNIE. *(Overlapping.)* Oh my gosh!

LUKE. *(Overlapping.)* Nuh uh!

PRESIDENT. *(Overlapping.)* What!

SHIVA. *(Overlapping.)* Ugh.

TOSCA. There was one extra space available after we had to send Armand home.

IFEZ. He was gorgeous.

TOSCA. So...please welcome...Jezebel!

> (**CAROL-ANN** *enters, dressed outrageously and in character.*)

CAROL-ANN. Hello. Boo ya.

ALIANA. Tell us about yourself, Jezebel.

CAROL-ANN. You think you guys are hot stuff? No. I am the real deal, people. I am a freaking legend. You haven't even heard of me because you haven't been worthy of hearing about me. How did I learn fashion? Um... I am fashion, fools. I started a studio at the age of four. While you creatures were playing dollies and dressing up your Barbies I was dominating the playground with my mind-destroying designs! I made my own clothes at six. I started my own YouTube channel at seven. I am awesome. And I'm not here to make friends, I'm here to kick fash. Un.

(Short pause.)

That's my catchphrase. Kick Fash. Un. Is there a way we can make T-shirts?

ALIANA. Thank you very much, Jezebel.

CAROL-ANN. Thank you! I'm gonna sit now!

ALIANA. Please sit.

CAROL-ANN. We're on the same wavelength. You and me, Aliana. Synchronized. Feels glorious, doesn't it?

ALIANA. Sit.

CAROL-ANN. Yes.

(She sits.)

TOSCA. It's time for the QuickSew challenge!

(Sound effect announcing QuickSew challenge. Perhaps an echoing recorded voice says, "QuickSew!")

When we return to the Project Design studio you will find a pile of garbage we pulled from a dumpster on 37th Street. You will have thirty minutes to create a fashion-forward accessory, using only yourself as the model. The winning designer will have immunity from elimination this round.

ANNIE. Wow!

PRESIDENT. It's the same thing every round Annie. You don't need to make exclamations.

ANNIE. Okay. Sorry.

PRESIDENT. You're always apologizing for yourself. It's sad.

ANNIE. Sorry.

TOSCA. And three two one...begin!

> *(Lights up on the Project Design studio, which is divided into tables and a sewing area. There are six mannequins located near the tables.)*

> *(There is also a large pile of garbage in the center of the room.)*

> *(At the beginning, the five designers sprint for the pile of garbage. **CAROL-ANN** is left in the dust.)*

CAROL-ANN. What is happening?!

> *(**SHIVA** grabs a hubcap from the pile.)*

> *(She stops and turns to the audience as the others scramble for garbage.)*

SHIVA. *(To the audience.)* I saw that hubcab first and I knew exactly what I was going to do. Necklace.

> *(**SHIVA** runs to her station and starts working.)*

CAROL-ANN. Who is she talking to?

ANNIE. The camera. You have to do confessionals to explain your thoughts.

CAROL-ANN. Aren't those recorded afterwards?

ANNIE. Nope.

PRESIDENT. *(To the audience.)* At first I went for the Arby's bag, but Ifez grabbed it. I will murder him.

> *(**PRESIDENT** runs over to his station.)*

ANNIE. When you feel the little electrical shock that means it's your turn.

CAROL-ANN. What?

> *(**ANNIE** steps forward to speak to the audience.)*

ANNIE. I haven't made any friends here. The pile of garbage reminded me of my life. But then I saw a wind chime and I thought about earrings.

(**ANNIE** *goes to her station.*)

(**CAROL-ANN** *feels an electric shock.*)

CAROL-ANN. Ah! What the heck?!

(*She gets shocked again.*)

Aah!

(*She starts swatting at imaginary bees.*)

Where the heck is it coming from?

ANNIE. It's under your skin. They implanted it during the interview process.

CAROL-ANN. Are you serious?

(*She's shocked again.*)

Ah! What! Fine.

(*She looks out at the camera.*)

The pile of garbage looked like garbage. So I grabbed... this...

(*She grabs a plastic bag filled with banana peels.*)

[Bag of crap.]* Which I will make into...a hat. Cool? Are we cool?

(*She waves at the camera then runs for her station, smashing into a mannequin and knocking it over.*)

Whoops. Sorry about that. This guy reminds me of my prom date. No hands.

(*Everyone else is working frantically on their objects.*)

PRESIDENT. Some of us appreciate silence.

CAROL-ANN. So you can plan. I got ya. Planning. Execution. Planning and execution.

IFEZ. Don't worry about President. He gets testy. He's so talented, he's like if Madonna and Cher had a baby.

---

*This line may be changed to "Bag of stuff."

Like some kind of tremendous alien baby where they combined two eggs and like cosmic rays hit it.

(**CAROL-ANN** *is staring at her bag.*)

CAROL-ANN. So.

IFEZ. I love to chat while I work.

ANNIE. Me too!

IFEZ. Shut up Annie! I hate her. So do you sweat? Do you like to sweat? I am like a fountain on camera. It's like Waterworld.

CAROL-ANN. Sure. So...

(*She looks at her bag of garbage. Takes out a banana peel.*)

(**LUKE** *comes forward.*)

LUKE. *(To the camera.)* I looked over at what Jezebel was doing. It was a nightmare.

CAROL-ANN. What?

(**TOSCA** *enters.*)

TOSCA. Five minutes remaining!

CAROL-ANN. Are you kidding me?! We just got in here!

(**TOSCA** *comes over.*)

TOSCA. I'm looking at your work right now...and I'm concerned.

CAROL-ANN. I know. I know.

TOSCA. I'm not seeing transformation.

CAROL-ANN. Right, well that's why –

TOSCA. And time's up! Please return to the runway.

(*Everyone else picks up their pieces, which are finished and look great.*)

(*Lights switch to the runway.* **ALIANA** *and* **TOSCA** *are waiting there.*)

ALIANA. Designers. Your task was to transform garbage into art.

(**CAROL-ANN** *raises her hand.*)

CAROL-ANN. Can I make a comment? We were supposed to have thirty minutes there, and I'm not entirely sure that was thirty minutes.

PRESIDENT. I thought you were going to dominate.

CAROL-ANN. I am dominating. Below the surface. But I also need time for domination. To dominate properly. You don't just show up at the dominatrix's place and expect her to be ready for you. She's gotta have time to prepare.

ALIANA. Let's see your work.

> (**SHIVA** *steps forward with her necklace.*)
>
> (*Everyone has completed their task and they look great. Use pre-prepared pieces.*)

SHIVA. I saw a hubcab and I thought about death.

CAROL-ANN. Any specific person's death or just death in general?

> (**SHIVA** *stares at* **CAROL-ANN.**)

SHIVA. Death.

CAROL-ANN. Like murder death or just sort of the natural process of aging?

ALIANA. Tell us about it, Shiva.

SHIVA. So when I think about death I think about choking. And strangulation. So I made a choker.

TOSCA. It's marvelous.

ALIANA. I love the story you created. So wonderful.

SHIVA. I would say thank you but I don't believe in thank yous.

TOSCA. I respect that.

ALIANA. Luke, what do you have?

LUKE. Well… At first I thought I saw a dead cat in there and I was like, I can't use a dead cat! No one can use a dead cat. Except Gandhi. Gandhi could probably do anything. But then I spotted some metallic food containers.

ALIANA. Oh!

TOSCA. Wow.

LUKE. So I merged them together, threaded some beads in there, and I made this handbag.

(He shows off a great purse.)

ALIANA. I feel like I've seen this before from you. You need to stretch yourself.

LUKE. Sorry. I'll try harder next time.

TOSCA. Ifez.

IFEZ. Hi.

TOSCA. You seem stressed. Breathe.

IFEZ. Okay. All right. Um... So... I hate this. Before I start.

TOSCA. No. You have to love your failures.

CAROL-ANN. That's what my mom says.

(They turn to look at her.)

About her other children. Probably not me. I didn't think that was about me. Until this moment here.

ALIANA. So what do you have for us?

IFEZ. Okay, so this is a bracelet I made from a used egg carton and French fries.

(It looks fantastic.)

I did a little crocheting here and I added these sparkly things to offset the saltiness of the fries.

ALIANA. I'm not feeling it.

IFEZ. I know. I know it's horrible. I'm gonna do better next time, I promise. It's just, you know, my head starts swimming and then I start thinking about the Disney Channel and my mind just goes to Miley Cyrus and I'm like, she's wasting her talent! She's wasting her talent! And then this happens. Can I cry now?

ALIANA. No.

IFEZ. I'll cry on the inside then. Like Miley.

ALIANA. You do that.

TOSCA. Annie.

ANNIE. Hi! I just want to say that I am grateful to be –

ALIANA. Whatever. What have you made?

ANNIE. Earrings! I found an old wind chime in the bag and I thought, I can do this! I'm a single mom, I can do anything! I raised three children and they are doing so well, so –

ALIANA. Are they?

ANNIE. Yes?

ALIANA. Are you sure?

ANNIE. I think so.

ALIANA. Well after I've seen those earrings I question your judgment.

ANNIE. Oh.

ALIANA. Someone call Child Protective Services! Ha ha ha. A little joke. I'm sure you're an adequate mother. And remember that your children's failings are not entirely your fault. Okay moving on.

ANNIE. So um...

PRESIDENT. Hi.

TOSCA. President.

(**PRESIDENT** *has an incredible furry jacket.*)

PRESIDENT. So I created this jacket, which isn't exactly an accessory, but my work is all about expanding pre-conceived notions. I reject the entire idea of a separation between accessories and pieces.

ALIANA. Wow.

TOSCA. What is this made out of?

PRESIDENT. Pain. And the skin of a dead cat I found in the bag.

LUKE. You didn't!

PRESIDENT. I did.

ALIANA. I love it. And I love the history it has.

TOSCA. It's really fashion-forward.

ALIANA. I feel like it's recycled material, and that's big right now.

PRESIDENT. Completely organic.

TOSCA. Nice work.

ALIANA. And finally... Jezebel.

CAROL-ANN. So...um... I made a hat.

> (*She puts the plastic bag of banana peels on her head.*)

As you can see...it's very avant-garde. If you don't like it you probably just don't understand it.

TOSCA. I feel like this is a summer piece.

ALIANA. I understand what you're trying to do.

CAROL-ANN. Do you?

ALIANA. And I applaud your risk-taking. It's kind of awful though.

CAROL-ANN. That's what I was going for.

ALIANA. I can see JCPenney's selling this.

TOSCA. Thank you designers! We will return in just a few moments with our decision.

ALIANA. I think I've got it.

TOSCA. Never mind.

ALIANA. Two pieces stood out for me today. Shiva. I enjoyed your choker.

> (**SHIVA** *nods.*)

And President – that dead cat jacket is winsome and macabre at the same time. And that's hard to make work. But there can be only one winner...and the person safe from elimination is...President.

SHIVA. What!

CAROL-ANN. ARE YOU KIDDING ME?! I WAS ROBBED!

ALIANA. You have the rest of the day to plot and engage in ill-advised romance. We'll see you tomorrow for the elimination challenge, when one of you...will be cut.

> (*Lights change.*)

> (*Lights up on* **CAROL-ANN** *talking into her phone.*)

CAROL-ANN. Day one. No one suspects me. I've narrowed the list of suspects to everyone in the room. And maybe the cameramen. They look shifty. Also, I was a little disappointed with my performance in the QuickSew – I'm gonna nail the next one. But it's time to go back to the hotel and do some major investigating. And that means the sensuous art...of seduction.

(IFEZ is right behind her.)

IFEZ. Who are you talking to?

CAROL-ANN. Siri. She's my only friend.

IFEZ. Oh.

CAROL-ANN. Do you have any friends, Ifez?

IFEZ. Well – I don't know –

CAROL-ANN. Would you like to be my friend?

IFEZ. Um... I'm sure you think you're a fantastic person –

CAROL-ANN. Oh I do think that.

IFEZ. But uh... I'm not interested.

CAROL-ANN. Your mouth says no but your funny little glasses say yes.

IFEZ. No they don't.

CAROL-ANN. They might.

IFEZ. I'm sorry but I've got a lot to work on for tomorrow.

CAROL-ANN. Tomorrow's a big day, huh?

IFEZ. It's the elimination challenge.

CAROL-ANN. Just like Hunger Games. Twelve people enter. One person lives. Somebody gets poisoned.

IFEZ. What do you mean, poisoned?

CAROL-ANN. Oh I don't know. Don't you think that's a way someone could die?

IFEZ. Why would anyone die?

CAROL-ANN. You seem nervous.

IFEZ. I'm always nervous.

CAROL-ANN. Why is that Ifez? You mind if I call you Fezzy? Fezzy Bear?

(She plays with his boa.)

I love your boa by the way. Most men aren't confident enough to wear boas. But I find it...fabulous.

IFEZ. Look, Jezebel –

CAROL-ANN. That's right, say my name.

IFEZ. Um...

CAROL-ANN. It's mysterious, isn't it? Jezebel. Kind of Biblical. Something about her in the Bible. Probably about disguises. But we all have our disguises, don't we, Ifez? How about we take those disguises off?

IFEZ. Nope! Nope. Look – you seem very nice, you need to be careful.

CAROL-ANN. Oh I'm always...

> *(She starts wrapping his boa around her own neck. She has a lot of trouble with it. It is very unsexy.)*

Careful.

IFEZ. There are people who would stop at nothing to win Project Design. That's all I'm gonna say. Nothing. I can't talk anymore! There's a lot of emotions swirling!

> *(He skitters off, crying.)*

CAROL-ANN. I still got it.

> *(Into her phone.)*

Chief Bailihew? Are you in?

> **(OFFICER JONES** *and* **OFFICER NIGELA** *enter on the opposite side of the room, on speaker phone.)*

OFFICER JONES. Officer Jones here!

OFFICER NIGELA. And Officer Nigela! In the house. Word.

CAROL-ANN. Where's the chief?

OFFICER JONES. I'm gonna level with you. He does not want to talk to you.

OFFICER NIGELA. No he does not. Word.

OFFICER JONES. He said, "Keep that crazy woman away from me. I'm going on a raft."

CAROL-ANN. He's going on a raft?

OFFICER NIGELA. That is what he said! And he seemed disturbed.

CAROL-ANN. All right look – I think I've got a lead –

OFFICER JONES. I'm gonna level with you. No one here believes in you.

OFFICER NIGELA. We're saying that in private. To each other.

CAROL-ANN. That's all the inspiration I need.

OFFICER NIGELA. We've started an office pool.

OFFICER JONES. When will she screw this up?

CAROL-ANN. I haven't even begun to screw things up, punks! You think I came here to fail? No, I came here to destroy, okay? And find the killer. Before he or she kills. And probably also find lasting love too, if Miss Congeniality is any guide to my life. Which it is! All right – I need some background info on these people. What can you tell me about Ifez?

   (Pause.)

What can you tell me about Ifez?

OFFICER NIGELA. Oh I'm sorry are you talking to us?

CAROL-ANN. Yes.

OFFICER NIGELA. I was playing Candy Crush on my phone. I was totally zoning out.

OFFICER JONES. It's so addictive. Like drugs. Which reminds me I have some things I need to take care of.

CAROL-ANN. I need to find out about a guy named Ifez. What's his real name?

OFFICER JONES. We're not really here to provide support, we're mostly here to make fun of you.

OFFICER NIGELA. But keep doing what you're doing! And if you could fail at four p.m. tomorrow that would be awesome.

   (Lights down on them.)

CAROL-ANN. All right then. Doin' this the hard way. Just the way I like it. In a non-sexual way. Kind of creeping myself out now. All right mister or miss potential killer, I'm coming for you. Check yourself.

   (She looks around, then exits.)

(Lights up on a room in the hotel. **SHIVA** *is sketching with her headphones in.)*

*(***CAROL-ANN*** *enters and watches her. She smells her breath and pops a breath mint. Then she takes a second one. She stretches out a bit, gathers her nerve, and approaches.)*

CAROL-ANN. He-ey. What is up?

*(***SHIVA*** *doesn't hear her.)*

How is it hanging? So we're gonna be roomies. Cool.

(She checks out the room awkwardly, probably bumps into something. **SHIVA** *ignores her.)*

You got your music. Listening to your tunes. Your iTunes. Or not iTunes if you're doing Spotify or whatever. That's cool. I'm not into judgments.

*(***CAROL-ANN*** *sits next to* **SHIVA**.*)*

I really liked your choker thing today. Way sexy. Like in a disturbing kind of violent way. But still, you know, hot. Smoking.

(She decides to try seduction.)

[I don't know which way your boat floats, but let me tell you, I'm all over the ocean. Any which way. So... maybe sometime...just the two of us – we could listen to music together – in some kind of industrial complex. That's probably your scene. Like an open furnace or something. Machinery. Probably a conveyor belt of some kind.]

(She makes a conveyor belt sound.)

[And we could just...you know...get industrial.]

(Alternate lines to the above lines in brackets are below.)

[I don't know if you're looking for friends here, but let me tell you, I am loyal. Supremely loyal. So...maybe sometime...just the two of us – we could listen to some tunes together – in some kind of industrial complex.

That's probably your scene. Like an open furnace or something. Machinery. Probably a conveyor belt of some kind.]

(She makes a conveyor belt sound.)

[And we could just play hopscotch or whatever... scandalize some Barbies.]

(End of alternate dialogue.)

SHIVA. Are you talking to me?

CAROL-ANN. *(Seductive.)* Do you want me to be talking to you?

SHIVA. I had my headphones in. I was ignoring you.

CAROL-ANN. Oh.

SHIVA. So I'm gonna go back to ignoring you.

CAROL-ANN. You can try, but I am a wide load of stimulation.*

> *(**CAROL-ANN** plays with **SHIVA**'s hair. Makes sound effects.)*

SHIVA. Do you have some kind of problem?

CAROL-ANN. Not anymore. Medication.

> *(**SHIVA** removes **CAROL-ANN**'s hand from her hair.)*

Right.

> *(**CAROL-ANN** steps away.)*

I'm just gonna do some yoga poses over here if you don't mind. I'm in a continuous state of yoga.

> *(She starts doing some yoga.)*

> *(**SHIVA** takes her headphones out.)*

SHIVA. I'm trying to do my sketching, okay? Tomorrow's going to be insane and I'm not getting cut. So go do your horrible yoga somewhere else.

---

*This line may be changed to "You can try, but I'm gonna friend you on Facebook."

CAROL-ANN. Sure. Sure. Can I ask you one question though? If you could kill one of the other competitors, which one would you kill and why? And please be specific in your answer.

SHIVA. All of them. Now get out.

CAROL-ANN. No doubt. But of course you'd probably want to eliminate the toughest competition, right? So that would be... President?

SHIVA. Ha. President is not who he says he is.

CAROL-ANN. His name's not President?

SHIVA. Let's just say I've known him for a long time. You'll find out.

CAROL-ANN. Bingo. And [if you change your mind about an awkward seduction, you'll find I am a bountiful lover.]*

(Lights up on **PRESIDENT** *and* **LUKE** *talking.)*

LUKE. He's totally imploding. It's sad to watch.

PRESIDENT. I used to like him. When we first got here I was like, "Oh, he's adorable, like a homeless puppy." But then like, he started designing and I was like, "Oh no, the puppy's got like one leg and eats its own vomit."

LUKE. Stop it!

PRESIDENT. I love talent, okay? Talent. Not whatever he's got. Legorrhea.

LUKE. What is that?

PRESIDENT. I don't know. Like diarrhea with legos.

LUKE. That sounds painful.

(They laugh.)

PRESIDENT. I thought you liked him.

LUKE. OMG no. Can you imagine that? Like meeting our friends? They'd be like, where did you get the garden gnome? Did you steal that off somebody's lawn?

PRESIDENT. You are awful! He's done some good work.

---

*This line may be changed to "If you change your mind about friendship, you'll find I am a glorious companion."

LUKE. Ugh. The bacon hat? That's all I have to say. Bacon. Hat. Like what is that? Who gets the food challenge and thinks, oh, this needs to go on my head?

PRESIDENT. At least it wasn't another tank top dress.

*(**LUKE** titters.)*

How many more half-naked women can he send down the runway? Like, tape is not a replacement for fabric, my friend. If you have to tape your tank top dress on, you have made terrible mistakes in your life.

*(**LUKE** titters again.)*

LUKE. I can't believe he's still here.

PRESIDENT. Can I be totally serious with you right now?

LUKE. Yes! I love it when you're totally serious.

PRESIDENT. You know who's the biggest threat?

LUKE. Me?

PRESIDENT. Shiva. She is fearsome.

LUKE. Don't worry about Shiva.

PRESIDENT. Why do you say that?

LUKE. She might be in for...an accident.

*(**CAROL-ANN** blunders in.)*

CAROL-ANN. What's up Homies?

(They look at her, offended.)

Homies. Homepeople.

PRESIDENT. Hi.

(Short pause.)

LUKE. Hi.

CAROL-ANN. So what's going on over here? Plotting? Right?

LUKE. Okay. I am feeling the need to not be here. Just because the vibe changed in a very unfortunate way. Also, I don't want to be photographed with you.

PRESIDENT. You don't need to announce your positions, Luke. We understand.

LUKE. Right. Okay.

CAROL-ANN. I'll catch up with you later.

LUKE. Oh. Honey no.

CAROL-ANN. But I'm gonna. You can't stop me. I'm like a tiger. I'm just gonna bust in places and wreck stuff.

LUKE. Tigers don't do that.

CAROL-ANN. They do.

LUKE. That's a misconception.

CAROL-ANN. It is not.

LUKE. You're stereotyping tigers. I know tigers. Okay? You're just using one for a wild metaphor and you don't know anything about them. It's offensive.

CAROL-ANN. I like you. I like your spirit.

LUKE. I have to leave. Okay. President. You're an inspiration.

PRESIDENT. Thank you.

LUKE. I mean it. You're my light in the darkness.

PRESIDENT. Great.

CAROL-ANN. He's like a tiger.

LUKE. Shut up about tigers!

(**LUKE** *leaves.*)

CAROL-ANN. He seems tense.

PRESIDENT. Luke's like that. He doesn't trust himself so he lashes out.

CAROL-ANN. What about you, President? Is that your actual name?

PRESIDENT. My mom was seeing all these people naming their babies Prince and Captain and whatever, so she was like, "Screw that, my baby's gonna be President."

CAROL-ANN. Wow.

PRESIDENT. My middle name's General. My second middle name's Pope. So I could be like General General Johnson or Pope Pope Johnson. If I choose that career path.

CAROL-ANN. I don't think Pope's a career path.

PRESIDENT. I don't limit my dreams. I'm just exploring right now. And then I'll choose one of those roles.

CAROL-ANN. Fashion designer's a good experience for Pope, probably. He wears that hat.

PRESIDENT. Can I tell you something? I love what you were doing with the banana peel garbage bag hat, but I just feel like you needed to iterate it one more time. Know what I'm saying?

CAROL-ANN. Definitely. I totally wanted to iterate it, but I ran out of time. For the iterating.

PRESIDENT. Yeah. That's sad.

(He steps out to talk to the audience.)

So Jezasmell or whatever just came to my room and was like talking to me, right? Like, what are you doing here? She is a trainwreck. I can't believe they let her on the show.

CAROL-ANN. I'm right here.

PRESIDENT. What?

CAROL-ANN. You just did a confessional and I'm right here.

PRESIDENT. We don't stop doing confessionals just because we're in the apartment.

CAROL-ANN. Yeah, but I'm right here. It's kind of rude.

PRESIDENT. It's kind of rude to point out somebody being rude.

CAROL-ANN. All right.

*(**PRESIDENT** steps out.)*

PRESIDENT. *(To the audience.)* Why is she arguing with me? Like, what do you want? And why is she wearing that? That rayon died for your sins.

*(**CAROL-ANN** takes a deep breath.)*

CAROL-ANN. So...um... I really liked your work today.

PRESIDENT. I'm sure.

CAROL-ANN. It was like really...real, like it had a realness to it.

PRESIDENT. I try.

CAROL-ANN. So...

(**CAROL-ANN** *feels the electric shock.*)

CAROL-ANN. Ow. So I was thinking...

(*She feels the shock again.*)

Ow – all right – ow –

(*To the cameras.*)

All right look I'm not going to do a confessional in the middle of a conversation! I'm not doing it! So just quit shocking me all right? We're talking here!

(*She waits for it. No shock.*)

So I was –

(*She gets shocked.*)

Fine. Fine!

(*She jumps up and talks into the confessional.*)

I love talking with President. He's so amazing and talented. Can I express my feelings for him? I sure hope so 'cause I need to get some loving! There! Are you happy? Satisfied?! Thank you.

(*She walks back to* **PRESIDENT**.)

Where were we? I was trying to seduce you.

PRESIDENT. Um... I don't know if you're picking up on my vibe or not, but –

CAROL-ANN. I don't care.

PRESIDENT. Right. And I respect that. But I think you might be barking up the wrong tree.

CAROL-ANN. [I'll bark up your tree all night long.]

PRESIDENT. Eww.

(**CAROL-ANN** *makes dog noises.*)

CAROL-ANN. Grr. Ruff.

(**PRESIDENT** *steps out.*)

PRESIDENT. (*To the audience.*) I'm having flashbacks to prom of my junior year. It is not going well. The whole time

I was like daffodil is not a color, it's an unfortunate accident of nature. Jezasmell is like a nightmare I had when I was six.

(He steps back in.)

(CAROL-ANN gets shocked.)

CAROL-ANN. What? Oh come on.

(She gets shocked again.)

(She steps out.)

President is a tough nut to crack. But I will crack him. I will crack him so good. Over and over again. There! You like that? You like that, do you? I'm trying to work my magic here, people!

(She gets back into it.)

So I've got an idea. We go in the closet.

PRESIDENT. I'm so done with the closet. I haven't been in the closet since –

CAROL-ANN. No I mean. You and me. Animal creatures. We go in the dark. Nobody can see each other. The cameras aren't watching. And you just tell Mama all your secrets.

PRESIDENT. Nope.

CAROL-ANN. I feel something between us. You feel it? There's a hunger between us.

PRESIDENT. Not really.

CAROL-ANN. [Oh yeah. This. This heat. You feel it. Underneath this exterior I am molten lava. I am a volcano. And I'm about to blow.]

(Short pause.)

That came out wrong. That's what he said.

PRESIDENT. Okay I'm just gonna back away now. You've loosed one too many double entendres.

CAROL-ANN. Oh I'm just started loosing the entendres.

PRESIDENT. Stop it. You are damaging my respect for the English language. Please. Please. I will get a hose.

CAROL-ANN. That's all right. I can take a hint. No need to get wet and wild.

PRESIDENT. Don't even finish your thought.

CAROL-ANN. I never do. Can I ask you a question though?

PRESIDENT. No I am not interested. I would rather make out with a duck.

CAROL-ANN. That was not my question.

PRESIDENT. Fine.

CAROL-ANN. How do you know Shiva?

PRESIDENT. What did she say?

CAROL-ANN. I'm just wondering. You two seem like you've got a history.

PRESIDENT. Lots of people have history. It's a small world.

CAROL-ANN. I got you. I know where you're coming from. Lots of people aren't what they seem. Right?

PRESIDENT. What do you want?

CAROL-ANN. I want to win. Okay honey? Rarr.

PRESIDENT. I gotta go.

> *(He runs off.)*

CAROL-ANN. *(Into her phone.)* Two suspects remain.

> *(**LUKE** walks across the stage.)*

LUKE. Don't even come near me devil woman!

> *(**LUKE** makes the sign of the cross at her and skitters away.)*

CAROL-ANN. *(Into phone.)* [One. Last. Seduction.]*

> *(Lights up on **ANNIE** talking in the confessional.)*

ANNIE. Really tough day with the QuickSew challenge. I'm trying to stay positive. It's tough though! All the other designers are really talented. I'm not sure what I think of the new girl.

---

*This line may be changed to "One. Last. Encounter."

(**CAROL-ANN** *sidles up behind her.*)

She's um...she seems nice.

CAROL-ANN. Really.

(**ANNIE** *laughs.*)

ANNIE. I didn't see you there!

CAROL-ANN. I'm everywhere. And I'm nowhere.

ANNIE. Wow.

CAROL-ANN. Yeah. Yeah wow. So what's your story, sweetheart?

ANNIE. Did you see my intro?

CAROL-ANN. I did, but I don't put a lot of stock in intros. Sometimes there's dark secrets just beneath the surface. You're a mom. You got three kids. You make clothes. I got that. But what I want to know is, why does everyone hate you?

ANNIE. I think they're just really catty.

CAROL-ANN. Uh huh. That would be the easiest explanation. But the easiest explanation is never the one I choose. But it looks like [you could use a friend in a platonic relationship that might have sensual overtones?]*

ANNIE. What?

(**CAROL-ANN** *gets buzzed and steps out.*)

CAROL-ANN. I was feeling something from Annie I haven't felt in a long time. Passion. Curiosity. Baked goods. I think we might have a winner in the Jezebel sweepstakes.

(*She steps back.*)

I'm gonna say something to you right now, and it's going to scare you. It's going to scare you like crazy. But underneath that fear there's going to be something cool as all get out – and it's an image of you and me and –

---

*This line may be changed to "You could use a friend in a disturbingly co-dependent relationship."

(High-pitched shriek from offstage.)

CAROL-ANN. Dang it.

(Lights up elsewhere onstage.)

*(**IFEZ** is standing and shaking, pointing at a pair of fabric shears that have lodged into a wall.)*

*(Everyone else, including **CAROL-ANN** and **ANNIE**, rushes in.)*

IFEZ. I was just standing here and the shears flew past my head! Like someone was throwing them at me! I was so close to death! It was horrible! There were little stars and I saw my life pass in front of my eyes and it was kind of great because I've lived fabulously but at the same time I'm really really frustrated with where I am right now and –

SHIVA. Shut up!

IFEZ. That is hurtful! I am undergoing trauma. Please respect my process.

(He starts hyperventilating again.)

I'm reliving it. Aaah.

*(**SHIVA** heads over to the shears.)*

SHIVA. There's a note attached.

IFEZ. It's a bomb!

SHIVA. It's a note.

(She takes it down, unfolds it, and shows it to everyone.)

"Your next."

LUKE. Me?!

SHIVA. It's not really assigned to anyone specifically.

PRESIDENT. Wait a minute, honey. Let me see that. Whoever wrote this didn't use an apostrophe. So I'm thinking this is a possessive. Your next something?

ANNIE. Your next what?

PRESIDENT. Your contribution is not appreciated, honey.

IFEZ. Can I have some comforting please?

LUKE. What if they meant you were going to be next? Like, you're the next one to die?

PRESIDENT. If they meant that, then they should've used an apostrophe to show a contraction. Come on.

IFEZ. What if they didn't know that rule?

(Everyone looks at IFEZ.)

When they wrote it? And tried to kill me with it?

SHIVA. Whoever wrote this wasn't concerned with proper grammar or clarity. We know that much. [Bastard.]*

LUKE. You don't know it was a man. It could've been a woman.

SHIVA. Look at this handwriting! You think a woman writes like this! You think a woman can't use an apostrophe correctly!

LUKE. Well you're just full of stereotypes tonight aren't you?! And isn't it convenient that you were the person to pull the shears out of the wall!

SHIVA. You're saying I did this?

LUKE. You think about death all the time!

SHIVA. That's because I'm stuck in this competition with you people! A nun would think about death all the time!

IFEZ. This is re-traumatizing me!

ANNIE. Can I make a suggestion?

IFEZ, SHIVA, LUKE & PRESIDENT. NO!

CAROL-ANN. All right muchachos. Let's all just simmer down a notch. Sure, someone just tried to kill Ifez, but even if the scissors had hit him, they probably would have just wounded him. I mean, there might be blood. I guess if they lodged right here in his back.

(She demonstrates on his back.)

I suppose they could have punctured the skin here, and then slid through his ribs and pierced his lungs.

---

*This line may be replaced with "Jerk."

That would cause a jet of blood to erupt from his back – spurting like a little geyser, right? Like blaaaah. And then Ifez would scream and probably be in excruciating pain – and that would only cause the scissors to wiggle back and forth –

IFEZ. I'm not feeling well.

CAROL-ANN. But the point is he missed.

LUKE. He! Again with the he! You're sexist! You are a sexist person!

CAROL-ANN. Fine! He or she or they! Happy?

LUKE. They?! Are you saying more than one person threw the scissors!

IFEZ. It's a conspiracy!

PRESIDENT. Luke, you're pretty, but you're also pretty dumb, so stop talking.

CAROL-ANN. I was using they as a singular gender-neutral pronoun.

SHIVA. I don't think you can do that.

CAROL-ANN. It's acceptable practice!

SHIVA. If only there was an English teacher here. We need an English teacher.

CAROL-ANN. What we know: Ifez was standing here, doing something.

IFEZ. Sometimes I stand.

CAROL-ANN. Okay. A person who might be any gender is standing over here and throws shears, with a confusing note attached to them, in a misguided and futile attempt to kill Ifez.

PRESIDENT. We're dealing with someone really incompetent.

CAROL-ANN. But strong. Because the scissors are thrown with enough force to penetrate the wall. Everyone make a muscle!

LUKE. No.

CAROL-ANN. Do it. I'll feel you all. Everyone let's go.

LUKE. I am not your puppet.

PRESIDENT. Come on. Flex everybody.

LUKE. Fine! This is degrading though. I'm not a piece of meat for your amusement. Although this is kind of like a dream I had anyway.

> *(Everyone flexes.)*

> **(CAROL-ANN** *goes from person to person and feels their arm.)*

CAROL-ANN. *(At* **SHIVA.***)* Nice.

SHIVA. Thank you.

CAROL-ANN. *(At* **PRESIDENT.***)* Disappointing.

PRESIDENT. What!

CAROL-ANN. *(At* **LUKE.***)* Somebody's spending time in the gym.

LUKE. I am naturally fit.

CAROL-ANN. I know you are.

> *(She moves to* **ANNIE.***)*

ANNIE. I was standing with you when it happened.

CAROL-ANN. I gotta be fair. I'm feeling everybody.

LUKE. Still like my dream.

> *(She feels* **ANNIE***'s arm.)*

CAROL-ANN. This one ain't doing it for me.

PRESIDENT. Hold on! You don't throw with just your arms. Any baseball player can tell you that! You use your lower body. What you're really looking for is someone with a strong butt.

CAROL-ANN. You're right. Line up.

LUKE. Oh come on!

CAROL-ANN. This is for science! I don't get any pleasure out of this. And neither will you.

ANNIE. Why don't we just call the police?

SHIVA. If we call the police, they'll cancel the show. No one will win. And besides they only tried to kill Ifez, it's not like they committed an actual crime.

IFEZ. That's *attempted* murder! That's a crime.

SHIVA. I don't see how you can be charged with a crime you didn't even succeed in committing.

IFEZ. It's a crime!

CAROL-ANN. It's really just an attempted stabbing.

IFEZ. That's still a crime!

CAROL-ANN. Eh. Maybe. All right let me feel your butts.

LUKE. This is ridiculous. Why are you the one doing this anyway?

SHIVA. Yeah!

CAROL-ANN. I took a class, all right? In design school. They had a crime-solving class. And I did well! And I have an alibi so you know I'm not the potential killer.

LUKE. Fine. But I don't like it.

CAROL-ANN. You don't have to like it. But right now I'm the only hope you've got. Bend over.

> (**LUKE** complies.)

> (**CAROL-ANN** moves behind each person and squeezes their butt.)

(At **SHIVA**.) Surprising.

> (She moves on to **PRESIDENT**.)

Wow. This is extraordinary.

PRESIDENT. I feel awkward.

> (She's still squeezing him.)

Are you done?

CAROL-ANN. I'll let you know when I'm done. Oh yeah there are some nice things going on here.

PRESIDENT. Are you done?

CAROL-ANN. Hold on!

> (She finishes, moves on to **LUKE**.)

LUKE. This is under protest.

CAROL-ANN. That's what they all say, honey.

> (She squeezes him.)

Eh.

LUKE. What?

CAROL-ANN. I mean it looks nice but when you get down to it...

LUKE. I wasn't flexing. I should be done again.

CAROL-ANN. Nope.

(She moves on to **IFEZ**.*)*

IFEZ. What? I'm the one they tried to kill!

CAROL-ANN. How do we know that?

IFEZ. Because the scissors went past my head!

SHIVA. So you say.

CAROL-ANN. Come to Mama.

*(***IFEZ*** reluctantly lets* **CAROL-ANN** *squeeze him.)*

Oh yeah.

IFEZ. Stop it!

CAROL-ANN. Annie?

ANNIE. I was next to you! I'm not dangerous!

PRESIDENT. That's a lie! She's a mother! That means she's capable of evil!

IFEZ. Yep.

ANNIE. Fine. Fine. Whatever.

*(***CAROL-ANN*** gives her a squeeze.)*

CAROL-ANN. Just as I thought.

PRESIDENT. What? What does that prove?

CAROL-ANN. Inconclusive. I'm gonna have to do it again.

(Everyone erupts in protest.)

THIS IS SCIENTIFIC!

(More protests from everyone.)

*(***PRESIDENT*** steps out to do a confessional.)*

PRESIDENT. This was getting us nowhere. Yes, someone tried to kill Ifez, but –

CAROL-ANN. *(Overlapping.)* Are you serious? Right now you're doing this?

PRESIDENT. *(Overlapping.)* [But we have an elimination challenge tomorrow. And if someone's gonna feel my butt all night long, he better be cute.]

LUKE. Holla!

CAROL-ANN. Oh shut up Luke.

LUKE. You are hurtful. And not in a good way.

SHIVA. President's right. The best thing to do is wait until the killer strikes again.

ANNIE. What? That's crazy!

PRESIDENT. Says the psychopath.

ANNIE. I'm not a psychopath!

PRESIDENT. THAT'S WHAT PSYCHOPATHS SAY!

CAROL-ANN. All right. We're not getting anywhere. Let's all go to bed and we'll meet tomorrow for the elimination challenge.

IFEZ. That sounds kind of bad. Elimination challenge.

SHIVA. Well, someone's getting eliminated, aren't they?

> *(Thunder.)*
>
> *(Lights change.)*
>
> *(Lights up on the runway.)*

LUKE. *(To the camera.)* So we were all a bit nervous from the attempted murder last night, but I was really excited for the elimination challenge, because OMG, we have special guest judges. And they are literally gods.

> **(PIETER** *and* **SAMANTHA** *step in.)*

SAMANTHA. Once again, I will be judging the elimination round, and I'd like to introduce our special guest judge –

PRESIDENT. Oh please. Like we don't know who this is.

SHIVA. You are amazing. You're everything.

IFEZ. I am like dying right now. Dying.

CAROL-ANN. Yep. Word.

> **(PIETER** *waves his hand slightly.)*

PIETER. Ya. Hello.

SAMANTHA. Pieter Van Omtrabben.

> *(**PRESIDENT, SHIVA,** and **IFEZ** give him a standing ovation.)*

PIETER. Ya. Again. I am...happy to be being here.

PRESIDENT. Oh my gosh yes. YES!

IFEZ. Can I touch you?

PIETER. No. I reserve that for the winner.

IFEZ. Okay.

SAMANTHA. So the elimination challenge today –

> *(Sound effect: A deep, echoing voice says "Elmination Challenge," followed by the sound of a slash and a scream.)*

CAROL-ANN. Um, hey, maybe we should change that sound effect so it doesn't sound like someone being murdered? Just throwing that out there.

SAMANTHA. So the elimination challenge today –

> *(The same sound effect plays again, followed by the slash and scream.)*

Is the Lock-In challenge!

> *(Sound effect of a prison door being slammed shut.)*

PIETER. Ya.

SAMANTHA. Pieter, could you explain the challenge?

PIETER. You think I am monkey? You say hop little monkey and I hop? No. I am Pieter. I do not hop.

SAMANTHA. It's on the teleprompter that you're supposed to introduce the challenge.

PIETER. Does the teleprompter own me? No.

SAMANTHA. Okay I guess I will take your lines then.

> *(She reads off the teleprompter.)*

Thank you Samantha I will introduce challenge now. Ya. The Lock-In Challenege! You have twenty-four hours to create an evening look for an ordinary woman.

PRESIDENT. Oh no. Ordinary women are horrible.

SAMANTHA. You will have twenty minutes to work with your ordinary models, and then you will be locked into the Project Design studios for twenty-four hours straight! Your only sustenance will be an unlimited supply of coffee! No one will be allowed in. No one will be allowed out. There will be no escape. Even in emergencies.

> (**CAROL-ANN** *raises her hand.*)

No phones will work.

> (**CAROL-ANN** *raises her hand more insistently.*)

We will periodically turn off the power and make you work in the dark to make things interesting.

> (**CAROL-ANN** *starts jumping up and down with her hand up.*)

What?

CAROL-ANN. Are you sure this is a good idea?

PIETER. What is good? What is bad? There is only greatness.

PRESIDENT. That's so deep.

IFEZ. Can I steal that?

PIETER. No.

IFEZ. Okay. Really excited by the way. Really excited. Nervous. Way too nervous. Probably going to have a stroke but I am ready for this. So ready.

SAMANTHA. You're shaking again.

IFEZ. I know. And if I could stop I would. But sometimes I just gotta keep going – you see the cliff and you're driving the car and you're like, "Hit the brake! Hit the brake!" But the brake doesn't work for you, you're just accelerating and you're going to die. Can we cut that part out in editing? We can cut that out right? You're gonna cut that?

SAMANTHA. If you don't make the cut, one of you...will be cut. And go!

(Lights up on the Project Design studio. There are six mannequins and tables again. Everyone rushes to their spot. **ANNIE** *speaks directly to the camera.)*

ANNIE. I so appreciate the opportunity to work with ordinary women. I mean, don't get me wrong, I love the models. It must be awesome to be a model and six feet tall and be able to look down on everyone and be like, "Worship me!" I'm sure they don't do that. I'm sure they have problems like everyone else. I don't know what they are, but they're probably worse than having three kids under the age of five and being broke and wondering where the child support went. I love my life. I really do. Love it. Sometimes I want to kill everyone and run away. Ha ha ha ha. I don't mean that. I have a sign in my kitchen. It's very inspirational. It says, "Don't kill everyone and run away."

*(**LUKE** steps forward.)*

LUKE. I immediately started thinking about color. And colors. Like a rainbow. That's like all the colors. So all I had to do was pick one and go with it. But then I thought about metallics. And I was like, "Are those even colors?" Because if they're not colors, then what are they? And I thought about that for a while. And then I thought, maybe someone gets murdered today. And then I decided to go with green.

(He goes back to his table.)

*(**CAROL-ANN** steps forward.)*

CAROL-ANN. So um... I'm freaking out a little bit. I decided on a full-coverage dress. Kind of like a tarp. You know, with uh...like straps and stuff. Because it's awesome and I'm awesome. So...my design is less of a plan than a mission statement. Pretty sure when the lights go out someone's going to end up dead.

(She steps back to her work station.)

IFEZ. *(To the audience.)* [I love my design. Really great sketching. Usually I'm like, "I hate it I hate it I hate it I hate it I kind of like it I love it I hate it." But today I love it right from the start! Probably 'cause someone is trying to kill me. Or this dress will kill me. Ha ha ha. Oh God.]

> *(He goes back to his work station, shaking.)*

PRESIDENT. Can I borrow someone's shears?

> *(Everyone looks at him.)*

What?

CAROL-ANN. Where are your shears?

PRESIDENT. ...I don't know. Can I borrow some?

> *(No one offers anything.)*

IFEZ. Why do you want them?

PRESIDENT. To cut some fabric. People. Are you serious right now? I didn't throw them at Ifez, if that's what you're worried about. And even if I did try to kill Ifez, I would use a different murder weapon with my second attempt. Like a needle.

> *(He holds one up.)*

SHIVA. Fine. I don't care. Here.

> *(**SHIVA** gives him her shears.)*

PRESIDENT. Thank you. You are brilliant.

SHIVA. You're welcome.

> *(She returns to her station.)*
>
> *(Pause.)*

CAROL-ANN. I'm just gonna circulate. Like the water cycle. Don't mind me.

> *(She picks up her mannequin and holds it like a shield between her and **PRESIDENT**.)*

PRESIDENT. Oh please. Any of us could have thrown those shears.

> (**CAROL-ANN** *considers it. She now keeps the mannequin between her and everyone. Moves over to see what* **IFEZ** *is doing.*)

CAROL-ANN. Cool. That looks like an alien.

IFEZ. Do you mind?

CAROL-ANN. Nope.

> (**CAROL-ANN** *takes* **IFEZ**'*s mannequin and holds it to her back.*)

IFEZ. Hey.

CAROL-ANN. You're not using it!

IFEZ. I'm going to use it!

> (**CAROL-ANN** *moves across the room with both mannequins.* **IFEZ** *scoots after her and snatches his mannequin back. He realizes he's away from his work station and holds his mannequin in front of him like a shield in order to get to her seat.*)

CAROL-ANN. Everyone just be cool okay!

> (*A mannequin falls over.*)

> (*Everyone jumps.* **IFEZ** *shrieks.*)

SHIVA. Sorry!

ANNIE. This is crazy, guys. It's just a competition. There's no need for murder.

LUKE. That's what Hitler said.

ANNIE. No it's not!

LUKE. I'm pretty sure he said that.

CAROL-ANN. Let's all just do our designs and –

> (*A buzzing sound interrupts her.*)

> (*The* **VOICE OF TOSCA** *comes over a speaker.*)

VOICE OF TOSCA. Designers. You now have five minutes to work with your models.

> (**BECKY** *and* **VANESSA** *enter awkwardly.*)

BECKY. Hi.

VANESSA. What's up?

> *(The designers stare at them.* **SHIVA,** **PRESIDENT, LUKE,** *and* **IFEZ** *all step forward to do a confessional. They take a moment, then get in line.)*

SHIVA. So there are two models. Two. For six of us. We have to share them.

> *(***SHIVA*** *goes back to her spot.)*

LUKE. I don't know much about ordinary women, but if these are ordinary women, I don't want to know anything more.

IFEZ. Mine is built like a hippopotamus. Seriously.

PRESIDENT. Like, don't you have any respect for yourself? You're like a size four. That's disgusting. And she's not even six feet tall. I don't know what to do.

> *(***PRESIDENT*** *goes to his table with* ***BECKY***.)*

> *(***VANESSA*** *stops in at the other tables.)*

BECKY. I've never been a model before.

PRESIDENT. I know. So these are the designs I made before I saw you, and now I'm just going to throw all that out the window, okay?

> *(He viciously crumples up his drawings and throws them over his shoulder.)*

And we're gonna start fresh. Like, when you go to Kohl's what is it you're looking for?

BECKY. Um...mostly just something that looks good.

PRESIDENT. Uh huh. And do you think you're succeeding with that? Don't answer. I'll just look at you for a moment. Drink you in, okay?

BECKY. Okay.

PRESIDENT. Just stand there and don't say anything. And if I start crying, they're inspirational tears. I always cry when I design.

> *(***PRESIDENT*** *looks at her. Thinks.)*

I'm just going to brainstorm now. So don't say anything. I'm going to throw out some emotions and images that occur to me, and I'll edit them later.

BECKY. That's a little weird but okay.

PRESIDENT. I didn't ask for comment. Okay...

(He looks at her.)

Apocalypse. Mad Max. Cannibals. Peach. Like a light tan. Murder.

*(**VANESSA** is at **CAROL-ANN**'s table.)*

VANESSA. I think I belong to you.

CAROL-ANN. Wow. Yeah. I'm digging this.

VANESSA. Thanks.

CAROL-ANN. So we are going to create something just mind-blowing for you.

VANESSA. Well I'm trying to find something tasteful –

CAROL-ANN. Don't even use that word. Someone says tasteful and you know what I think? Snooze. Snoozefest. No. We are not going to be tasteful. We are going to be...amazing. Like, how do you feel about Wonder Woman?

VANESSA. I don't know.

CAROL-ANN. That's okay. 'Cause I know how I feel about her. She's a personal hero of mine. Whenever anything happens I think, WWWWWD. What would Wonder Woman do? WWWWWD. Just four Ws. I get that messed up sometimes. It makes me go crazy! All right. You know what Wonder Woman does most times?

VANESSA. She fights?

CAROL-ANN. She ties people up. With ropes. How about it?

VANESSA. I'm a little scared.

CAROL-ANN. Me too. But that's what fashion is about. Being afraid. All right let's Kick Fash! Un.

*(**CAROL-ANN** steps out.)*

No idea what I'm going to do. Making stuff up.

(**BECKY** *approaches* **SHIVA**'s *table.*)

BECKY. I think I'm supposed to be assigned to you too.

SHIVA. You know sometimes you think the universe hates you? I was right.

(**LUKE** *comes over.*)

LUKE. Actually I think you're supposed to be with me.

VANESSA. I think I'm with you.

LUKE. Let's switch.

SHIVA. I'm fine actually.

LUKE. I really think my style would work better with a more attractive woman.

VANESSA. What?

LUKE. Honey. This is not about self-deception. This is about fashion. You're perfect for Shiva. She makes beautiful women look hideous, so she might do the opposite for you.

SHIVA. Luke, use your own model.

LUKE. I hate this one.

SHIVA. Tough.

LUKE. You are always like this! You just want to see me fail!

IFEZ. Guys, we're running out of time.

ANNIE. Yeah can we speed it up?

LUKE. Why are you being combative, Annie? This isn't about you. Go ahead and stay at your table and work on your puritan dress!

ANNIE. I'm not making a puritan dress! I was thinking about –

LUKE. No one cares!

SHIVA. Use your own model, Luke!

LUKE. This is so not fair! This is a tragedy! She's got gorilla shoulders! How am I supposed to design for gorilla shoulders!

VANESSA. I don't have gorilla shoulders!

LUKE. I could put one regular model on each of your shoulders! It's insane!

IFEZ. Hurry up we're almost out of time!

LUKE. OMG Ifez deal with it!

IFEZ. You deal with it!

LUKE. Give her to me!

SHIVA. I will cut you, Luke. I have knives and I will cut you!

CAROL-ANN. Okay, well maybe let's not threaten to –

LUKE. I'm not scared of you! I do Pilates! Bring it on!

IFEZ. Come on!

(**PRESIDENT** *sees the design on* **LUKE**'*s table.*)

PRESIDENT. Wait a minute, did you copy my design?

LUKE. No!

PRESIDENT. This is my design!

LUKE. I'm adapting it!

PRESIDENT. You can't take my design!

SHIVA. You are a dumpster fire of a human being!

IFEZ. I hate you!

LUKE. None of you understand me! I'm a misunderstood genius!

(*A timer rings.*)

VANESSA. So that means we need to go.

BECKY. This was really um…offensive. So I'll see you later.

ANNIE. What!

IFEZ. No!

(**BECKY** *and* **VANESSA** *leave.*)

I didn't even get a chance to work with her!

LUKE. She didn't seem all that cooperative.

IFEZ. Now I'm not going to get a chance to see what looks good on her and I'm going to end up with something horrible and everything is going to fall apart –

LUKE. Someone's overreacting.

IFEZ. *You. You did this.* I will destroy you.

LUKE. You're just jealous because I'm prettier than you.

IFEZ. Argh.

LUKE. I can't help it if you look like a troll hobbit.

>(**IFEZ** *attacks* **LUKE** *with a mannequin.*
>**PRESIDENT** *tries to hold him back.*)

>(**LUKE** *gets his own mannequin and starts
>swinging back.*)

You think you can take me! I do Tae Bo!

>(**CAROL-ANN** *gets between them.*)

CAROL-ANN. STOP THE MADNESS! Someone's gonna get –

>(**LUKE** *smacks her with a mannequin.*)

Hurt.

LUKE. Sorry. I just can't stand it when you talk.

IFEZ. I'll kill you!

LUKE. Not if I kill you first!

ANNIE. I'LL KILL ALL OF YOU!

>(*Everyone stops and looks at* **ANNIE.**)

Metaphorically. Probably.

>(*The lights go out.*)

SHIVA. AAAAAH!

LUKE. WHAT IS HAPPENING?!

PRESIDENT. THEY TURNED OUT THE LIGHTS!

CAROL-ANN. NOBODY MOVE!

>(*Everybody moves.*)

>(*The lights come up suddenly.*)

>(*Everyone is holding a mannequin in front
>of them like a shield.*)

>(*They stare at each other.*)

Everyone still alive?

>(*They all count with their fingers. Everyone
>is still alive.*)

VOICE OF TOSCA. Hello designers.

IFEZ. AAAH!

VOICE OF TOSCA. We'll be turning out the lights again at different points tonight. Just to keep things interesting. Like this.

> *(The lights go out again.)*

CAROL-ANN. NOT COOL!

> *(Scrambling noises as everyone moves again.)*

I MEAN IT PEOPLE! STOP MOVING AROUND!

PRESIDENT. NO!

CAROL-ANN. LET'S ALL BE PEACEFUL, DANG IT!

> *(The lights come up suddenly.)*

> *(Everyone is carrying a weapon and a mannequin.)*

> *(They stare at each other. Count again. Everyone is still alive.)*

> *(TOSCA enters.)*

TOSCA. Hello designers.

> *(Everyone puts their weapons behind their backs and heads to their tables.)*

Ifez. How are things?

IFEZ. I'm a little stressed right now.

TOSCA. You always seem a little stressed.

IFEZ. Yeah, but right now it's a little more than normal.

> *(PRESIDENT steps out to do a confessional.)*

PRESIDENT. And then Tosca was there. He's like a mischievous sprite. I love him. Still, I was feeling pretty great that I had immunity.

TOSCA. Annie. How are things with you?

> *(The lights go out again.)*

CAROL-ANN. WOULD YOU STOP DOING THAT?!

> *(More movement.)*

> *(Lights up suddenly.)*

(Everyone looks around. Counts.)

*(They all get to **TOSCA**, who is lying on the floor, dead.)*

(Pause.)

*(**CAROL-ANN** steps forward.)*

So then Tosca was murdered.

(Lights down.)

End of Act One

ACT TWO

(Sound effect of a cheesy television show, Fashion Assault. Lights up on **BLAIZE** *and* **UMA**, *the two hosts.)*

BLAIZE. Welcome back to the Fashion Assault! Where we rate the developments in the fashion universe for the week with military precision!

UMA. Ten-hut!

BLAIZE. And I'm here as always with my partner in crime, Uma. I love you, Uma. Really do.

UMA. Thanks.

BLAIZE. Totally over our last fight.

UMA. Me too. I am not harboring any resentments for you even though I don't think you're talented.

BLAIZE. Great. So what's new this week?

UMA. Well, we're all tuning into Project Design this week. And we had this look from President. What do you think?

BLAIZE. I don't know what I'm supposed to think.

UMA. I never know what I'm supposed to think. With this, though, I'm like...this reminds me of death.

BLAIZE. Yeah.

UMA. Like my dog could wear this and pull it off, you know?

BLAIZE. I'm sure. Your dog can pull off a lot of looks.

UMA. He totally can. He's brilliant.

BLAIZE. Absolutely. He's an inspiration to other dogs.

UMA. I think he is. I really do.

BLAIZE. Sure. Except he's a loser.

UMA. What.

BLAIZE. You have a totally unrealistic opinion of your dog. I've met him. I was not impressed.

UMA. Don't talk about my dog.

BLAIZE. He should just give up. Go in his little dog house and turn on the car and kill himself, right? Who's with me, studio audience? Do you know Uma's dog?

UMA. The studio audience hates you and everything you stand for.

BLAIZE. The producers are whispering in my ear that we need to talk about Project Design again.

UMA. Holla!

BLAIZE. You sound old when you do that. That was like four years ago.

UMA. It was not.

BLAIZE. That was like a zombie comment. You raised that comment from the dead and now it's wandering around trying to eat the living.

UMA. Your mother must be really proud of you. Part-time host on a fashion show.

BLAIZE. Thank you, she is.

UMA. I mean, most normal mothers would probably be pretending you died in a fire or something, but your mom probably has a photo of you in her house.

BLAIZE. How many husbands have you gone through?

UMA. One less than you.

BLAIZE. So... Project Design, what do you think of the other designers?

UMA. Normally I hate watch it. But this season is delicious.

BLAIZE. I know.

UMA. Don't agree with me. I didn't ask you to agree with me.

BLAIZE. I'm just making a comment.

UMA. All right. Make your comments.

BLAIZE. I did.

UMA. Okay. Great. The world is a better place now. Are you happy? Did you bring peace on earth?

BLAIZE. Let's talk about Ifez.

UMA. He's adorable. He's like a stray puppy. I just want to take him home.

BLAIZE. He'd probably jump off a cliff if he came to your house. He'd meet your dog and be like, "I have to die."

UMA. New Girl. Jezebel.

BLAIZE. Yes.

UMA. How did you feel about her garbage bag hat?

BLAIZE. Honestly, it excited me. I want to see what direction she's going in.

UMA. Yeah. That sounds like something you would say.

BLAIZE. It was. Because I said it.

UMA. I know you said it. I'm not surprised you said it.

BLAIZE. And that's all the time we have for today!

UMA. You screwed that up.

BLAIZE. No I didn't.

UMA. Yes you did. I can read the teleprompter too. It's not like a special skill set you have, you know.

BLAIZE. All right fine.

UMA. Can I do my tag? 'Cause it's written on my teleprompter.

BLAIZE. Do it. [It's like what your ex-husband said when you were taking all those pills.]

UMA. All right then. Well I can't wait to see what happens on Project Design next! There's gonna be fireworks! I'm ready for the elimination!

> (*Lights out.*)
>
> (*The actor playing* **BLAIZE** *runs over and becomes the dead* **TOSCA***.*)
>
> (*Lights up suddenly on the Project Design studio.*)
>
> (**IFEZ** *is in mid-freak-out.*)

IFEZ. AAAAAAAAAAHHHHHHH!

ANNIE. Are you sure he's dead?

IFEZ. I DON'T KNOW! AAAAAAAAH!

CAROL-ANN. CHILL OUT! CHILL THE HECK OUT! STOP IT! STOP IT! STOP SCREAMING! I'LL KILL YOU!

IFEZ. AAAAAAAAAAH!

CAROL-ANN. I DIDN'T MEAN IT!

LUKE. Think happy thoughts!

IFEZ. What?!

LUKE. Happy thoughts! Think happy thoughts!

IFEZ. Okay...

> (**IFEZ** *thinks happy thoughts.*)

Oh that is better.

PRESIDENT. All right everybody quit freaking out. There's a logical explanation for this.

SHIVA. Someone killed him.

PRESIDENT. No. Maybe it's a coincidence. Maybe he had a heart attack.

> (**SHIVA** *approaches the body. She kicks it.*)

SHIVA. He seems dead.

PRESIDENT. I know that! But we don't know what caused him to die!

IFEZ. He was *murdered*!

CAROL-ANN. All right back off! Let me look at him.

> (*She looks at the body closely.*)

I can't tell.

> (*Everyone groans.*)

SHIVA. Wait!

> (**SHIVA** *finds something on the body.*)

Hot glue. There's hot glue on his skin.

PRESIDENT. Is it hot?

LUKE. Why does everything have to be hot with you?

PRESIDENT. No is the glue still hot?

SHIVA. Why would it still be hot?

CAROL-ANN. All right back off! I'm gonna sniff it! I have a brilliant nose.

(Everyone watches as she sniffs the hot glue.)

Poison.

LUKE. Whoah.

CAROL-ANN. Hold on. I've got the scent.

(She tracks the hot glue to one of the stations, where she finds a hot glue gun.)

Lookee here. Boom.

ANNIE. So he touched it here? And then it killed him?

SHIVA. Poisoned hot glue.

PRESIDENT. Who was using the hot glue?

(Everyone looks at **IFEZ.***)*

IFEZ. Don't look at me! All right fine I was using it, but why would I poison my own glue?

CAROL-ANN. Why do you do anything? No one knows!

IFEZ. Someone poisoned my glue to kill me, idiot!

CAROL-ANN. Just like someone supposedly "threw" the shears at you?

IFEZ. Yes!

ANNIE. Okay, I have a good idea.

PRESIDENT. You haven't had a good idea since you've been here.

*(***LUKE** *high-fives* **PRESIDENT.***)*

LUKE. Good one!

PRESIDENT. I know. Zing.

CAROL-ANN. What's your idea?

ANNIE. No one else touch the hot glue.

SHIVA. And?

ANNIE. That's it. No one else touch it. Because it's poisoned.

LUKE. That is a good idea.

*(***PRESIDENT** *groans.)*

IFEZ. So who had access to my glue?

PRESIDENT. [Honey, everyone's had access to your glue. Just no one wanted it.]

LUKE. Oh!

(**LUKE** *high-fives* **PRESIDENT** *again.*)

That was like a double entendre.

CAROL-ANN. All right shut up with your clever wordplay! Ifez has a good question. Who had access to his glue and wanted access to his glue because he or she didn't have standards?

(*No one laughs.*)

Oh come on you laughed for him.

LUKE. It was already played.

SHIVA. I'm already disappointed by you.

CAROL-ANN. Ifez, where did you get the glue gun?

IFEZ. It was in my station.

CAROL-ANN. Okay.

ANNIE. Should we like tell someone about this?

CAROL-ANN. Is your phone working?

ANNIE. No.

CAROL-ANN. Can you open the doors?

ANNIE. No.

CAROL-ANN. Do you think the producers are watching right now?

ANNIE. No.

CAROL-ANN. There you go.

(**ANNIE** *steps out.*)

ANNIE. So um...hello producers. If you're paying attention and haven't just automated this show...we've got a bit of a situation – Tosca is dead, and there's someone in here trying to kill us. So um...if it's not too much trouble, maybe you could let us out and call the police or whatever. Okay? Anyone listening? Call the police maybe? People in here are going to die. Most of us. Most of us will probably be dead soon.

(No response.)

SHIVA. They don't care. It'll probably increase ratings.

LUKE. Maybe this is part of the show. Anyone ever seen Hunger Games? Like, only one of us is getting out of here alive.

(Pause.)

IFEZ. That's crazy.

LUKE. And they've like, hypnotized us into thinking that we're actually fashion designers and implanted false memories in our brains, but really we're just tribute children engineered for their amusement?

IFEZ. Ha ha.

> *(**IFEZ** picks up a sewing needle and holds it in front of him.)*
>
> *(Everyone else slowly picks up weapons.)*

CAROL-ANN. People! This is insane!

PRESIDENT. It's what Tosca would have wanted. A fight to the death. The real elimination challenge.

SHIVA. I'm game.

ANNIE. Bring it.

> *(They start circling each other.)*

PRESIDENT. Hold on. If we're really gonna do this, I still have immunity.

SHIVA. No way!

PRESIDENT. I don't think that's fair. I won immunity – no one should be able to kill me. Let's vote on it.

CAROL-ANN. Whoah. No! No. Stop the madness.

> *(She gets in the middle of the circle.)*

I know I'm new to this game, but you know what I see from all of you? Love. Mostly of yourselves, but also of other people.

ANNIE. Thank you.

PRESIDENT. Must you open your mouth?

CAROL-ANN. There's a better way. We don't have to all kill each other.

IFEZ. Ooh! I know. We keep doing the twenty-four-hour challenge and pretend nothing happened.

LUKE. I like that. I like that a lot. We use our imagination.

CAROL-ANN. What? Tosca is dead!

LUKE. I don't know that. I'm wishing it away with my imagination.

(*ANNIE steps forward.*)

ANNIE. At first I thought Ifez's idea was crazy. Someone just died. We should stop the competition and go home to our families and our beautiful children screaming and hitting each other in our tiny houses with our student loan debt and never be on television again. And then I thought, we still have twenty-two hours left in this contest.

(*She steps back in.*)

Okay.

SHIVA. Deal.

PRESIDENT. Awesomeness.

(*Everyone looks at* **CAROL-ANN.**)

IFEZ. What do you say? We just imagine this didn't happen and keep going? Please?

ANNIE. It would mean a lot to me.

CAROL-ANN. I'm staring at a dead body.

IFEZ. We can fix that!

(**IFEZ** *and* **LUKE** *take* **TOSCA***'s body and drag him into the closet.*)

There! Tosca who?

(*The body falls out of the closet.* **IFEZ** *shoves him back in.*)

CAROL-ANN. Whoever killed him is still in this room.

(*Everyone looks around.*)

And they probably didn't kill the person they wanted to kill. So we have an incompetent murderer in our midst, who will most likely strike again. And I will be ready to stop him or her with my mad judo skills when he or she strikes again. Boom.

IFEZ. So you're in?

CAROL-ANN. Heck yes!

(PRESIDENT steps out.)

PRESIDENT. Of course we could stop the competition and figure out who the murderer is. We could do that. And then the whole show will be over and no one will win the award and no one will prove that they're the best designer. We could do that. But then again, is that what Tosca would have wanted? I can imagine him now, in his little Tosca voice, "Make it work." I figure that means, "Even if I'm killed by poison, make it work."

(Lights change.)

(IFEZ steps out.)

(Lights fade a bit upstage.)

IFEZ. The hardest part about the twenty-four-hour challenge is staying awake. I found the fear of death was really helpful in that. And also the free coffee. Which I supplemented with my secret supply of Rockstar.

(He produces a can of Rockstar.)

So much caffeine in this. I like Rockstar because I feel like I'm a rock star when I'm on it, you know? Like the kind of rock star that's going to trash a hotel room and throw a television out the window. That kind. So we all settled in with our coffee coffee coffee and it was so... sparkly.

(Lights back up to full.)

(Everyone is working really fast.)

ANNIE. Ten hours left!

LUKE. You already said that three minutes ago!

ANNIE. I jumped the gun. Now I mean it.

SHIVA. I cannot work like this. I can't. Who cares how much time is left? I don't care. I'm working here – I HAVE WORK TO DO.

(*She downs her coffee in one gulp.*)

IFEZ. Bi bi bi bi bi bi bi bi –

SHIVA. Stop it stop it. Stop the noises. Stop it.

IFEZ. Bi bi bi bi bi bi bi –

CAROL-ANN. Hey does anyone know how to sew? I'm not really a sewer. I'm more of a conceptual artist thing. This is like waking dreams, right? Okay. Nobody? Anyone want to help me with the sewing machine? Anyone? 'Cause I can just keep talking until someone comes over here. I got all night people. My vocal cords are lubricated and I can talk for hours. Anyone? That's cool.

(**CAROL-ANN** *stares at the sewing machine.*)

Does anyone know where the power switch is?

(**IFEZ** *comes over and points to her power switch.*)

Sweet.

(**SHIVA** *has made her way to the coffee machine.*)

SHIVA. Who didn't refill the coffee?

(*No one answers.*)

Someone didn't refill the coffee. I REPEAT: SOMEONE DID NOT REFILL THE COFFEE MAKER. Do we have videotape? Can we find out who did this? WHO HAD THE LAST COFFEE? WHEN YOU EMPTY THE COFFEE IT IS YOUR OBLIGATION TO REFILL THE COFFEE. THOSE ARE THE RULES OF HUMANITY.

(**SHIVA** *starts making more coffee.*)

PRESIDENT. I'm pretty sure it was Ifez.

IFEZ. What?

SHIVA. You think I won't kill you? You think you're going to live through this night? I will murder you, Ifez, I will split you open and I will suck the sweet caffeine from your blood. You understand me? I will kill you.

ANNIE. I think maybe it was President who didn't refill the coffee.

SHIVA. What?

LUKE. Word.

CAROL-ANN. So how do you make the thread go in the fabric? It doesn't seem like it wants to do that.

SHIVA. I will get to the bottom of this. And when I discover who it was, watch your back. I'm not above going to prison. I'll do fine there.

> *(She goes back to the coffee.)*

Whoah.

CAROL-ANN. What?

> (**SHIVA** *pulls a dead scorpion out of the coffee pot.)*

SHIVA. Look.

PRESIDENT. What is that?

SHIVA. A scorpion. Someone put a dead scorpion in the coffee.

IFEZ. AAAAAAAAH!

CAROL-ANN. Oh come on that wasn't even close to killing you! How does a dead scorpion hurt anyone?

LUKE. Poison.

CAROL-ANN. It's dead! You can't poison someone with a dead scorpion! At least I don't think so.

IFEZ. Maybe it was a live scorpion and the coffee killed it.

LUKE. Ohhhh. Yeah. Huh.

ANNIE. Ooh I know! The killer is trying to kill again! Wow.

CAROL-ANN. So we're dealing with a killer who can't use an apostrophe correctly, who poisoned the wrong hot glue, and who thinks a scorpion can survive in coffee. We're dealing with a stupid, stupid person.

(Short pause.)

ANNIE. It could be any of us.

*(**BECKY** and **VANESSA** enter.)*

BECKY. Hi there!

IFEZ. AAAH!

PRESIDENT. Stop it!

CAROL-ANN. Whoah. Are the doors open?

VANESSA. They said we had fifteen minutes to meet with the designers –

IFEZ. Who did? Who's they?

VANESSA. The producers?

IFEZ. We're trapped in here. This is a death trap. People are trying to kill us.

BECKY. What? Should we leave?!

IFEZ. Um...well maybe after the competition's over 'cause we're running out of time.

VANESSA. You could probably get out now.

IFEZ. Nah I'm cool. Just repressing some things. And besides I didn't even get to work with you last time!

PRESIDENT. All right ladies. I have some gorgeous designs that –

IFEZ. You got them last time! I get my model first!

*(**IFEZ** escorts **VANESSA** to his station.)*

VANESSA. Is there something happening?

IFEZ. Don't worry about it. I have something fantastic to show you and it's going to make all your emotional problems disappear. Maybe not all of them.

*(**SHIVA** takes **BECKY**.)*

VANESSA. I don't think I have emotional problems.

IFEZ. Ha ha ha ha! You are adorable. And I love that about you. Your imagination. And that's what my clothes are about. Imagination. We are imagining a new and better you that is still appropriate. Sometimes I imagine myself as all kinds of crazy things and then it's like aaaaah shut down the brain! Shut down the brain! I do that sometimes because I need to take a break from the voices, right? I'm sure you know all about it. Okay and Ta-Da!

(He produces his dress.)

Do you love it? You love it right? You love it?

VANESSA. Um...

IFEZ. You hate it. It's a nightmare. It's the worst thing you've ever seen.

VANESSA. No.

IFEZ. It's somewhere in the middle. It's neutral. It's Switzerland.

VANESSA. I guess.

IFEZ. That's great because I wanted to change this completely anyway and I've got at least like eight and a half hours to come up with something completely new! I love it. I love the challenge. I am going to die alone.

*(**ANNIE** swoops in on **BECKY** and takes her away from **SHIVA**.)*

ANNIE. Hi I didn't get a chance to talk to you before because of sexism.

BECKY. Hi.

ANNIE. Okay. Well I have something fantastic for you.

BECKY. Actually I think I'm supposed to be working with –

CAROL-ANN. Come to Mama.

ANNIE. Um I haven't had a chance yet to work with the models so I only think it's fair to –

CAROL-ANN. You can have her when I'm done. Come on. I've got such sights to show you. You ever seen that movie? Hellraiser?

BECKY. No I don't think so.

CAROL-ANN. That's what Pinhead says before he takes you to hell. Which prepares you for my fashion.

BECKY. Wow.

CAROL-ANN. Oh yeah.

> (**CAROL-ANN** *produces her dress, which is an absolute mess.*)

It's not done. Put it on.

BECKY. I don't think I can.

CAROL-ANN. They'll blur out the nudity when we're on TV. All right do it do it do it –

ANNIE. Maybe I could talk to Vanessa?

LUKE. Nope! Mine mine mine.

> (**LUKE** *takes* **VANESSA** *away from* **IFEZ.**)

> (**BECKY** *is struggling to get into* **CAROL-ANN***'s disaster.*)

My inspiration was color. And it's glorious. How do you feel about rabies? As a concept?

VANESSA. For my clothes?

LUKE. It's not about clothes, honey. It's about life. And diseases.

> (**BECKY** *has the dress on, as best she can.*)

BECKY. Okay. Um...

CAROL-ANN. It's upside-down. That's all right. We'll work with it. This is a concept piece and the concept is –

> (*The lights go out.*)

AW COME ON!

PRESIDENT. WHAT IS IT THIS TIME?

CAROL-ANN. YOU KNOW THE DRILL PEOPLE! NOBODY MOVE!

> (*Everybody moves.*)

I HEAR YOU! I HEAR YOU MOVING! STOP IT!

LUKE. I'M TOO PRETTY TO DIE!

VANESSA. Is something wrong?

IFEZ. NOPE! JUST A LITTLE PANIC!

    (Whump! Someone hits the ground.)

CAROL-ANN. That didn't sound good. Did someone just get killed? It sounds like someone got killed!

BECKY. SOMEONE GOT KILLED?!

CAROL-ANN. It's not you obviously, don't worry about it. Everybody FREEZE!

    (More movement.)

    (Lights up.)

    (Everyone is hiding under their tables except **CAROL-ANN.**)

ANNIE. Is everyone all right?

CAROL-ANN. I'm pretty sure someone's dead.

    (One by one, they all come up from behind their desks.)

IFEZ. Oop! It's this one.

    (**IFEZ** *drags* **VANESSA***'s body out from behind* **CAROL-ANN***'s desk.)*

BECKY. Vanessa?!

PRESIDENT. Oh that's her name. I was trying to remember it.

SHIVA. Vanessa's dead?! Dang it!

    (Everyone looks at **SHIVA.***)*

I mean, what a senseless tragedy. Because the killer was obviously trying to kill someone else.

CAROL-ANN. Everyone stand back! She could still be dangerous.

    (**CAROL-ANN** *investigates.*)

BECKY. This is awful! I didn't know her well, but we were talking backstage and getting to know each other! She had a beautiful soul, I could tell that right away.

CAROL-ANN. Her beautiful soul's all over the floor. Smashed in the head with a blunt object. Like a sewing machine.

PRESIDENT. She was at your station! She's behind your desk!

CAROL-ANN. Well I didn't do it! I don't even know how to use a sewing machine!

LUKE. You picked it up and you bashed her over the head with it!

CAROL-ANN. You're delusional. Someone snuck over here in the dark, picked up the sewing machine...they were trying to kill me. Someone was trying to kill me!

PRESIDENT. Honey, if someone was trying to kill you, it would be to prevent you from completing your work. The world has enough pain.

BECKY. I can't believe Vanessa's dead. She was telling me about her dreams – how she was in love with a guy but wasn't sure he wanted to commit because –

PRESIDENT. Let's put her in the other closet.

IFEZ. Right.

*(**IFEZ** drags her toward a closet.)*

BECKY. What are you doing?

IFEZ. It's a standard procedure. When someone gets killed, we hide the body. Don't ask me, I'm not responsible!

BECKY. What! Call the police! This is a crime scene!

SHIVA. It's kind of been a crime scene already.

BECKY. But this is crazy! Someone died and you kept working?!

PRESIDENT. Success is ten percent inspiration and ninety percent perspiration. At least I've heard that. I don't sweat because of a laser procedure I had a while back, though.

BECKY. That doesn't have anything to do with this!

PRESIDENT. Helps me stay fragrant. Totally worth it.

BECKY. She's dead! And someone else is dead! And the killer is right here!

LUKE. Maybe you're the killer.

BECKY. What?! Why would I be the killer?

LUKE. Usually the person who protests the most is the killer.

CAROL-ANN. Maybe I can put this in perspective. You know about World War II, right? Fighting the Nazis?

BECKY. Yes?

CAROL-ANN. Okay, so it's D-Day. We're storming the beach at Normandy. Somebody next to you gets shot. Do you stop and go, "Oh no, someone killed Private Johnson! Let's figure out who killed him"? Or do you buckle down and keep going up that hill?

(Short pause.)

BECKY. I'm not sure what World War II has to do with –

CAROL-ANN. Greatest generation, all right? They did things. Even though people were getting killed left and right. They didn't have seat belts or food labeling or common sense. But they did it. Just like we're making clothes and filming this reality show.

BECKY. She's not making any sense. Right? She's not making any sense, is she?

IFEZ. Is she?

SHIVA. All truth is relative.

BECKY. This is crazy!

CAROL-ANN. The terrorists win if we stop. This is America. We keep going, even when it doesn't make any sense to do so.

LUKE. [Hell yeah!]

BECKY. I'm sorry I can't do this! We have to stop the show! I'm telling the producers!

(They move to stop her.)

PRESIDENT. Honey. Honey. This is reality television. It's more important than the lives of people who aren't famous.

BECKY. Get away from me!

ANNIE. Seriously, you get to wear all the clothes.

BECKY. No! No! No!

(She grabs the hot glue gun off IFEZ's station.)

BECKY. Stay back! You guys are like zombies! We're getting the police in here and we're figuring this out! Before anyone else gets killed!

LUKE. You might not want to hold on to that –

BECKY. What?

(*She looks at the hot glue in her hands.*)

Ohhhhh...

(*She passes out.*)

(*Everyone stares at her.*)

(*Pause.*)

SHIVA. Well she wasn't even murdered.

IFEZ. Other closet?

PRESIDENT. Yep.

(**IFEZ** *and* **LUKE** *drag her body to the other closet.*)

ANNIE. Y'all mind if I do a confessional?

LUKE. Go for it.

(**ANNIE** *steps out.*)

ANNIE. So with both of our models dead I needed to think fast. I'll have to adjust the sizing on my dress to fit myself, which shouldn't be too difficult. On the plus side, this puts us all on equal footing again. I'm feeling pretty good about my design.

(*She steps back.*)

(*Everyone looks at her.*)

We're going back to work, aren't we?

(*Everyone rushes back to their station and starts working again.*)

(*Lights change.*)

(**LUKE** *does a confessional.*)

LUKE. We made the decision to use ourselves as runway models. Since we don't have any left. And there's a big difference between designing for a man and designing for a woman. Luckily, my model was super manly, so it didn't change my design much. I think she was on steroids. Seriously.

(**CAROL-ANN** *does a confessional.*)

CAROL-ANN. I decided not to use the sewing machine. I'm going for more of a rustic look. I also discovered duct tape. And I can use that stuff on anything. It's a real industrial-type thing, and I'm just gonna tape this sucker all over my body. Also –

(*She takes a moment and takes out her phone.*)

I am working very hard on the case and I've almost got it solved. Just about. Just so you know I have done nothing wrong.

(**PRESIDENT** *steps forward.*)

PRESIDENT. The last hour is always the worst. People are running around like maniacs. It smells like sweat and hot glue and failure.

CAROL-ANN. (*In the background, working frantically.*) Aaah! Aaaaah! Aaaah!

PRESIDENT. (*Continuous.*) Especially near me because I'm between Annie and Ifez, and that is like the Bermuda Triangle of failed designers. I look over at Annie and it is a disaster. It is like some kind of Fidel Castro religious prophet thing – And then Ifez...he's like a little animal that's been killed and eaten by a larger animal. You feel bad, but then like...that's nature, right? He exists so that he may be eaten by other creatures. And then –

(**LUKE** *puts his dress up to his body and models it.*)

(*It is exactly the same as* **PRESIDENT**'s.)

(**PRESIDENT** *steps back into the scene.*)

What is that?

LUKE. My dress.

PRESIDENT. Are you sure? 'Cause it looks like my dress.

> (**PRESIDENT** *gets his own dress, which is identical.*)

MAYBE MY EYES ARE DECEIVING ME! BUT THESE LOOK SIMILAR!

LUKE. They're not the same dress.

PRESIDENT. THEY ARE THE SAME DRESS!

LUKE. MINE HAS A PATCH! SEE? SEE?! Do you see the patch?!

PRESIDENT. That's a patch –

LUKE. That's my style! That's my signature style!

PRESIDENT. Give that to me!

LUKE. No!

PRESIDENT. Give it to me!

LUKE. Nooo!

> (**PRESIDENT** *chases after* **LUKE** *to take his dress.*)

> (**LUKE** *tries to throw a mannequin at* **PRESIDENT**, *but* **PRESIDENT** *gets the dress.*)

Aaaaah!

PRESIDENT. Ha!

> (**PRESIDENT** *rips off the patch.*)

Now it's my dress!

> (**LUKE** *loses it, clutching his head with both hands.*)

LUKE. AIEEEEE!

IFEZ. Whoah.

> (**LUKE** *grabs* **IFEZ**'s *dress.*)

LUKE. Now this one's mine!

IFEZ. Hey! Give that back!

LUKE. I HAVE BEEN AWAKE FOR TWENTY-THREE HOURS AND I HAVE HAD SEVENTEEN CUPS OF COFFEE AND THERE ARE THREE DEAD

BODIES IN THE CLOSET AND I AM NO LONGER THINKING RATIONALLY! GIVE IT BACK TO ME OR I WILL KILL THIS DRESS!

IFEZ. Whoah!

> (**IFEZ** grab's **SHIVA**'s dress.)

Then I'm killing this one!

SHIVA. Give it back now or I will kill you.

IFEZ. Okay.

> (He gives it back and grabs **ANNIE**'s.)

Then I'm taking Annie's!

ANNIE. Then I'm taking this one!

> (She grabs **SHIVA**'s dress.)

SHIVA. I'll kill you!

ANNIE. I HAVE THREE KIDS I'M NOT SCARED OF DEATH!

SHIVA. Fine! Then I'm taking...

> (She looks at what **CAROL-ANN** has made.)

Um...

CAROL-ANN. You can take mine, I don't care.

SHIVA. It's just... Um...

CAROL-ANN. Mine's way outside the box.

SHIVA. Yeah. Um...

> (She snatches **PRESIDENT**'s original dress.)

PRESIDENT. Ah!

IFEZ. Let's everyone calm down!

LUKE. I want my dress back or I'm adding shoulder pads to this!

IFEZ. You monster!

> (**LUKE** runs to grab stuffing.)

No! Fine this one gets a plunging neckline!

> (He runs to grab his scissors.)

ANNIE. Ah! Then I'm putting see-through panels in this one!

SHIVA. And I'm adding stupid patches to this one!

PRESIDENT. Then I'm drawing an unironic smiley face on this!

(Everyone is ready to strike.)

CAROL-ANN. And I'm... I'm doing... Seriously no one wants to hold my dress hostage? Really?

(She holds it up.)

(The lights go out.)

REALLY? ALL RIGHT NOBODY – WHATEVER – EVERYONE RUN AROUND THEN!

(Boom! Smash!)

(A struggle.)

IFEZ. Someone touched me inappropriately!

CAROL-ANN. Whoops!

PRESIDENT. *(Overlapping.)* I HAVE IMMUNITY! REMEMBER I HAVE IMMUNITY!

SHIVA. *(Overlapping.)* Wait! Aah!

LUKE. Stay away from me I'm a black belt in Zumba!

PRESIDENT. Give me that dress!

LUKE. No!

SHIVA. AAAAAARGGH!

(Lights up.)

*(**SHIVA** has a sewing needle stuck in her shoulder.)*

IFEZ. AAAAAAAH! She's dead!

SHIVA. I'm standing up moron!

ANNIE. What happened to you?

SHIVA. What do you think?! Someone stabbed me with a sewing needle!

PRESIDENT. I'll help pull it out.

SHIVA. No.

IFEZ. I think you should leave it in there. If you take it out, blood'll just spurt all over the place. Gross.

LUKE. You could incorporate it into your outfit.

PRESIDENT. Ooh. Love it.

SHIVA. Arrrhghg... I'm not incorporating it into my outfit!

LUKE. If you had one in the other side it would work better –

PRESIDENT. I'd put the second needle on the same side, just slightly lower.

SHIVA. No one's putting any more needles in me!

PRESIDENT. All right, but it would be totally hardcore.

SHIVA. Someone just tried to kill me!

CAROL-ANN. They failed though. That fits the pattern. That's their fifth attempt.

PRESIDENT. Whatever you want to say about the killer, I admire their tenacity.

ANNIE. Definitely. So hard these days. Sometimes people just give up.

SHIVA. I am in pain!

PRESIDENT. Use it!

SHIVA. Aarrrrghg!

PRESIDENT. Good!

*(****CAROL-ANN*** *grabs the needle.)*

CAROL-ANN. Here!

(She pulls on it, it doesn't come out.)

SHIVA. Aarrgh!

CAROL-ANN. Let me try again.

(She pulls again.)

SHIVA. Arrghggh!

CAROL-ANN. Whoops. Here get down.

*(****CAROL-ANN*** *pushes* ***SHIVA*** *onto the ground. She grabs the needle with both hands, and puts one foot on* ***SHIVA****'s head.)*

*(****ALIANA*** *enters.)*

ALIANA. Good Morning Des–

> (**CAROL-ANN** *yanks the needle free.*)

CAROL-ANN. Gotcha! A ha!

> (*She holds the bloody needle aloft and turns to see* **ALIANA** *behind her.*)

He-ey.

ALIANA. –Igners. I trust you had a productive night.

ANNIE. (*Overlapping.*) Definitely.

IFEZ. (*Overlapping.*) Sure.

SHIVA. (*Overlapping.*) Arrgh.

Well, to be honest with you, there've been a couple of murders. But not to worry because –

LUKE. (*Interrupting.*) I'VE FIGURED IT OUT!

CAROL-ANN. (*Interrupting, a little late.*) I've figured it out! Actually – hold on a second –

> (**LUKE** *gets in front of her.*)

LUKE. I've been lying to you all. My name isn't Luke Burbank. It's Jackson Collins, NYPD.

> (*He shows his badge. Gasps from everyone.*)

I've been deep undercover on this show to –

CAROL-ANN. Oh come on, what!

LUKE. It was just like Miss Congeniality. My assignment was to go undercover and find out the killer. But what I didn't count on, was falling in love.

ALIANA. I love it.

CAROL-ANN. Time out.

LUKE. Annie, I wanted to let you know that –

ANNIE. I'm not interested.

LUKE. Shiva, I wanted to let you know that –

SHIVA. I'm emotionally unavailable.

LUKE. Jezebel, I wanted to let you know that I have feelings for you. Which is why it's so hard for me to say this: You're the killer.

(Gasps from everyone.)

PRESIDENT. I knew it!

ANNIE. And I trusted you!

CAROL-ANN. Whoah. Pause. Time out. Game over. First off, [Jackass]* –

LUKE. Jackson.

CAROL-ANN. Whatever. *I* am the police officer. *I'm* the one who's undercover. And I'm the Sandra Bullock character! You don't even look like Sandra Bullock! You'd look ridiculous in a dress! [Plus, I'm the one falling in love with the killer, which is easy for me, since I swing in all directions!]

LUKE. Where's your badge?

CAROL-ANN. It's um...

(She searches herself for her badge.)

I uh... I have it in my hotel room.

LUKE. And if you're a police officer, then why didn't you stop things before three people got killed?

ALIANA. Three people were murdered?

PRESIDENT. Give or take. Honestly, we're not sure if the last girl is dead or not, we just put her in the closet.

CAROL-ANN. Because I'm not very good at my job, all right? I'm a loose cannon! I don't play by the rules! Except for the rules to this show, which I followed, and you'll find my design is awesome. Also, when these go down the runway, you're gonna blur out the nudity, right? Because mine is really obscene.

ALIANA. I'm not sure what –

CAROL-ANN. I'm digressing. Listen, No-Action Jackson, I have been studying the situation for a good thirty hours now, and I know exactly who the killer is!

LUKE. Sure. Because it's you.

CAROL-ANN. It's not me!

---

*This may be replaced with "Loser," "Jackoff," or "Donkey."

ALTERNATE ENDING #1 (ANNIE)

ANNIE. Then who is it?

CAROL-ANN. Oh I think you know who it is.

(She walks toward **ANNIE.**)

LUKE. Can you not do the I-figured-this-out walk please?

CAROL-ANN. Oh I'm doing the walk.

LUKE. And you're not even a cop!

CAROL-ANN. I'm more cop than you'll ever be! Now, sit down, shut up, and let the big girls take care of things!

ALIANA. I like your spunk.

CAROL-ANN. THANK YOU. Now, I'm gonna back up and do the walk again. Annie, if you could say that again please.

ANNIE. Say what again?

CAROL-ANN. What you just said.

ANNIE. What did I say?

CAROL-ANN. You said, "Then who is it?"

ANNIE. Oh. Then who is it?

*(**CAROL-ANN** does the walk again.)*

CAROL-ANN. Oh I think you know the answer to that question.

LUKE. She's not even doing the walk right.

CAROL-ANN. First question: who threw the scissors at Ifez? It wasn't me, it wasn't Annie. There was only person with the arm and buttock strength necessary to throw those shears. President.

PRESIDENT. Ah!

CAROL-ANN. You screwed up, Buddy. You mentioned the word baseball. None of the rest of these people have any idea what baseball is. Because you're no fashion designer.

LUKE. He's a cop too?!

CAROL-ANN. Nope. What's his real name? Annie, I think you know it. You went to high school with him.

ANNIE. His name's Billy.

PRESIDENT. No!

CAROL-ANN. Thank you. And I also happen to know he has a wife and two kids and lives in Edina, Minnesota.

PRESIDENT. You're wrong! I'm a visionary! I'm amazing!

CAROL-ANN. Shhh...and I know Annie made you throw those scissors. She was going to expose you, wasn't she? BECAUSE ANNIE IS THE KILLER!

ANNIE. You don't know anything!

CAROL-ANN. You put the poison in Ifez's glue. You blackmailed President into planting the scissors. You don't know anything about scorpions or apostrophes! You bashed Vanessa on the head by accident when you figured out I was on to you, and you stabbed Shiva just 'cause you're mean.

IFEZ. I knew I didn't like her!

ANNIE. Fine. Fine. You got me. I'm here to win. And I'm not going back!

(She grabs **ALIANA** *and the hot glue gun.)*

Everyone stand back!

ALIANA. This is unacceptable.

ANNIE. You don't have any idea what it's like in my house! We watch Caillou every day! Have any of you people ever seen that show?!

(Everyone shakes their head.)

None of you have children, that's why. Any of you see Barney? Dora the Explorer?

LUKE. Oh yeah sure.

ANNIE. Those shows are like War and Peace compared to Caillou! Caillou is like what happens when someone takes sandpaper to your eyeballs. It's about this boring little French kid and he does nothing! He does nothing! He just sits there and mumbles stuff! So I was watching the show and I'm thinking, "If I have to kill someone to get out of this, I will." And that's when I got the call from Project Design! I know I'm not as good as the rest of you! I know they were going to send me home! Home to Children's Television! I'm not going back! I'm getting my designs in Marie Claire magazine and the grant to start my home design studio or Aliana dies!

ALIANA. You're cut.

ANNIE. You're about to be cut even more!

PRESIDENT. Annie. Please, if our friendship means anything –

ANNIE. It doesn't!

PRESIDENT. But if it did –

ANNIE. It doesn't!

CAROL-ANN. Hold on. I think I can do this. It's just like Miss Congeniality.

ANNIE. What is?

CAROL-ANN. This whole thing. Because that's how I really knew who was the killer. You and me.

ANNIE. What?

CAROL-ANN. Don't deny it. We work together, girl. We're like Peanut Butter and Jelly. I'm crunchy and you are sweet and a little slimy.

ANNIE. Stay back Jezebel!

CAROL-ANN. You don't want to hurt Aliana. You didn't want any of this. You just want a different cable plan where you don't have to watch Calliou.

ANNIE. You don't know anything!

CAROL-ANN. I know one thing. You're really bad at killing people.

>   (**CAROL-ANN** *charges.*)

Rarrrrhghggh!

ANNIE. Aaaaaaaaah!

ALIANA. Aaaaaahah!

>   (*Bonk!* **IFEZ** *hits* **ANNIE** *in the back of the head with a mannequin.*)
>   (**ANNIE** *collapses.*)

IFEZ. Whoops.

LUKE. I always hated her.

SHIVA. She was the worst.

PRESIDENT. Thank goodness that's over.

ALIANA. There are three dead people in the closet.

PRESIDENT. ...Yeah. We made some poor choices. But we're continuing the show right?

ALIANA. One of the hosts is dead.

SHIVA. But did he really matter? I mean, you're the star of the show.

ALIANA. Thank you.

PRESIDENT. I've got an idea. We tie Annie up, put her in the closet, and then go to the runway.

ALIANA. That's crazy.

> *(Short pause.)*

But that's what we do here on Project Design.

> *(Cheers from everyone.)*

> *(They drag* **ANNIE** *off.)*

> *(***CAROL-ANN*** steps forward.)*

CAROL-ANN. What did I say? Domination. Mic drop.

> *(Short pause.)*

Can I get a mic? For the mic drop? Is there a way? Are we still rolling?

> *(Lights down.)*

End of Play

> *(During the curtain call, it would be great if the actors could come out on the runway modeling their looks.)*

ALTERNATE ENDING #2 (IFEZ)

IFEZ. Then who is it?

CAROL-ANN. Oh I think you know who it is. Bob.

IFEZ. What?

CAROL-ANN. That's right. Bob. This guy here, he's a good actor, he wears his little boa, his little clunky shoes, his funny glasses, oh sure...says his name is Ifez...but where's he from? No one knows. I'll tell you where he's from! Indianapolis!

(Shock from everyone.)

IFEZ. I don't know what you're talking about! You're crazy!

CAROL-ANN. What was the one thing every murder had in common?

PRESIDENT. They were poorly executed?

CAROL-ANN. Okay there's that.

ANNIE. They were dumb?

CAROL-ANN. Also true, but still not what I'm looking for.

SHIVA. They displayed a complete lack of competence.

CAROL-ANN. Guys, these are all kind of the same thing! No, the real thing they had in common was this guy right here! The shears were next to his head, it was his glue, he was close to my station, and he had access to scorpions!

LUKE. How?

CAROL-ANN. I'm glad you asked. Because Bob here is not a fashion designer, he's a lepidopterist!

(Shocks from everyone.)

PRESIDENT. I don't know what that is.

IFEZ. You're so stupid. A lepidopterist studies butterflies. Everyone knows a scorpion is an arachnid and someone who studies them is an arachnologist.

CAROL-ANN. Got ya! Only an arachnologist actually knows what an arachnologist is! Ha ha!

IFEZ. Ah!

ALIANA. You caught him!

IFEZ. Fine. You got me.

ANNIE. But why?

IFEZ. You're asking me why I came on this show and tried to kill all you people?

ANNIE. Yeah.

IFEZ. Do you know any famous arachnologists? You don't, do you?!

PRESIDENT. If only I could Google one –

IFEZ. You can't! Yes I enjoyed the company of arachnids! Yes I enjoyed going to schools and terrifying school children with spiders in boxes! That was fun! But it never gave me what I wanted. What every American wants: Stinking stinking fame. I didn't just want a spread in Marie Claire, I wanted to be on the cover of Us magazine and Star and National Enquirer and all those other horrible tabloids! I wanted it all! I wanted to be hated on Twitter! And I would kill to get there! So I came up with an idea sure to win me fame. Become the most hated person on a reality TV show. So I came on this show, sure that Ifez would be the most despised character ever. But guess what? You were still more hateful than me! Everyone hated you people more! So there was only one solution: murder. And I can still do it!

(He charges at **CAROL-ANN.***)*

Aaarrrgghgh!

CAROL-ANN. Bring it!

(Bonk! **LUKE** *hits* **IFEZ** *in the back of the head with a mannequin and he collapses.)*

ANNIE. If it makes you feel any better, I hated you.

SHIVA. He was the worst.

PRESIDENT. Thank goodness that's over.

ALIANA. There are three dead people in the closet.

PRESIDENT. ...Yeah. We made some poor choices. But we're continuing the show right?

ALIANA. One of the hosts is dead.

SHIVA. But did he really matter? I mean, you're the star of the show.

ALIANA. Thank you.

PRESIDENT. I've got an idea. We tie Ifez up, put him in the closet, and then go to the runway.

ALIANA. That's crazy.

> *(Short pause.)*

But that's what we do here on Project Design.

> *(Cheers from everyone.)*

> *(They drag **IFEZ** off.)*

> *(**CAROL-ANN** steps forward.)*

CAROL-ANN. What did I say? Domination. Mic drop.

> *(Short pause.)*

Can I can get a mic? For the mic drop? Is there a way? Are we still rolling?

> *(Lights down.)*

End of Play

> *(During the curtain call, it would be great if the actors could come out on the runway modeling their looks.)*

ALTERNATE ENDING #3 (SHIVA)

SHIVA. So who was it?

CAROL-ANN. Oh I think you know who it was.

SHIVA. No I don't know who it was, that's why I asked.

CAROL-ANN. Oh I think you know.

SHIVA. No I don't.

CAROL-ANN. Yes you do.

SHIVA. Pretty sure I don't.

CAROL-ANN. Pretty sure you do.

> *(She turns out.)*

Who was the most emotionally disturbed person here?

> *(Everyone points at someone else.)*

No, seriously, if you think about it, who was the most disturbed person here?

> *(Everyone points at **CAROL-ANN**.)*

Oh come on!

LUKE. I'm just going by what I see.

CAROL-ANN. Shiva. It was Shiva!

SHIVA. What!

ANNIE. Oh. That's sad.

SHIVA. Trust me, if I tried to kill you people, I would've succeeded.

CAROL-ANN. I suppose that's true, if you were actually trying to kill the other competitors. But you weren't, were you? Ifez was never your target. He's not a threat to you.

IFEZ. Oh come on!

PRESIDENT. He's right.

CAROL-ANN. You killed your model because you stood a better chance of winning if you modeled your own clothes and you didn't like her body type.

SHIVA. Ridiculous.

CAROL-ANN. And you killed Tosca because he knew who you really were.

SHIVA. Who am I then?

CAROL-ANN. Well, I just happened to find this little nugget: Your audition video.

SHIVA. No!

CAROL-ANN. Ooh someone's a little feisty now.

(We hear SHIVA's voice recorded.)

SHIVA'S VOICE. *(Recorded.)* Hi there! I'm Sally and I love making clothes!

SHIVA. TURN IT OFF!

CAROL-ANN. Oh it goes on like that for a while.

SHIVA'S VOICE. *(Recorded.)* You know what I really love, the Bedazzler!

SHIVA. Aaaaagh!

CAROL-ANN. Tosca had to die because he knew your true identity.

LUKE. So she stabbed herself?

SHIVA. It wasn't that hard. Fine, you got it right. I did it. I set up Ifez to make it look like him. I intentionally misspelled the word "you're" because I figured he was an idiot who couldn't use an apostrophe correctly.

IFEZ. Hey!

SHIVA. Silence!

IFEZ. Okay.

SHIVA. I found the scorpion in Annie's suitcase –

CAROL-ANN. I was wondering where that came from.

PRESIDENT. Why did you have a scorpion?

ANNIE. My children are terrible.

PRESIDENT. That doesn't really explain –

ANNIE. Don't judge me!

SHIVA. So I put it in the coffee, knowing it would die and it would deflect suspicion. And yes, Tosca knew my terrible secret. I am not the designer you think I am. I am a mild-mannered housewife.

ANNIE. Ooh! We could be friends!

SHIVA. Never! The producers said they already had one pathetic middle-aged woman on the show and couldn't have two. So I came up with the idea of becoming Shiva, Goddess of Destruction. At first I only wanted to last a few weeks, but then, after I started doing well, it occurred to me: if I won, I could be Shiva all the time. But they'd never let me. They were going to kick me out this week. So...murder was the only option.

CAROL-ANN. Well Sally, looks like you needed a new option. Hey-O! But why record a death threat and send it to the police?

ALIANA. Oh that was the producers. We do that from time to time to increase ratings. It's actually our promo for the week.

CAROL-ANN. All right boys. Drag her off.

PRESIDENT. I'm not dragging her off, I'm still scared of her.

IFEZ. I'm incapable of physical exertion.

LUKE. Nuh uh.

CAROL-ANN. You're a cop!

LUKE. But I'm not a good one.

> *(Wham!* **ANNIE** *smacks* **SHIVA** *on the back of the head with a mannequin and knocks her out.)*

ANNIE. Moms don't have time for nonsense.

PRESIDENT. Thank goodness that's over.

ALIANA. There are three dead people in the closet.

PRESIDENT. ...Yeah. We made some poor choices. But we're continuing the show right?

ALIANA. One of the hosts is dead.

ANNIE. But did he really matter? I mean, you're the star of the show.

ALIANA. Thank you.

PRESIDENT. I've got an idea. We tie Shiva up, put her in the closet, and then go to the runway.

ALIANA. That's crazy.

>(*Short pause.*)

But that's what we do here on Project Design.

>(*Cheers from everyone.*)

>(*They drag* **SHIVA** *off.*)

>(**CAROL-ANN** *steps forward.*)

CAROL-ANN. What did I say? Domination. Mic drop.

>(*Short pause.*)

Can I get a mic? For the mic drop? Is there a way? Are we still rolling?

>(*Lights down.*)

End of Play

>(*During the curtain call, it would be great if the actors could come out on the runway modeling their looks.*)

ALTERNATE ENDING #4 (PRESIDENT)

PRESIDENT. Then who is it?

CAROL-ANN. Oh I think you know who it is.

PRESIDENT. Ha ha. Why do you say that?

CAROL-ANN. I don't know. Why do I say that?

PRESIDENT. That's what I'm asking you.

CAROL-ANN. Why do you think you're asking me?

PRESIDENT. I don't know what you're saying.

CAROL-ANN. Why don't you know what I'm saying?

PRESIDENT. What?

CAROL-ANN. Oh yeah.

PRESIDENT. What?!

CAROL-ANN. That's right.

PRESIDENT. Stop it!

CAROL-ANN. Confess!

PRESIDENT. Okay! I did it! YOU GOT ME!

LUKE. Wow.

ANNIE. That was incredible.

IFEZ. She deserves a raise.

CAROL-ANN. Tell 'em what you did.

PRESIDENT. It was supposed to be fun at first. I didn't think it would get out of hand. I just wanted to scare Ifez. Make him crack.

IFEZ. But why? You had immunity!

PRESIDENT. It was never about immunity! It was about keeping up the illusion that I was coming up with my own designs! You see I...I...copied off of Luke.

LUKE. I knew it!

PRESIDENT. My name's not President. It's Stanley. I was fooling all of you.

SHIVA. I knew it.

PRESIDENT. I know you knew. Which is why I tried to kill you. But I've never been good at anything! My whole life! I wasn't good at baseball, I wasn't good at soccer, I wasn't good at macramé –

CAROL-ANN. What's macramé?

ANNIE. It's where you glue things on –

PRESIDENT. Do you mind? I'm in the middle of my explanation! And I was awful at killing people! I tried to kill Shiva four times and I missed every time!

SHIVA. Stanley!

PRESIDENT. Sorry. You had to die because you knew the truth about me. I kept Luke alive because he's actually the best designer here and I needed someone to copy from –

LUKE. Thanks.

IFEZ. Oh come on.

PRESIDENT. It's true, Ifez. And now, now I go back to my life as an Uber driver.

ANNIE. I hear that pays well –

PRESIDENT. It doesn't! And I don't like other people and they keep getting in my car. And every time I'm like, get out of my car! And then I get low ratings on the app and it's a whole nightmare.

(**PRESIDENT** *breaks down.*)

CAROL-ANN. Well now you're just gonna have to be bad at being in prison. 'Cause you're going downtown.

PRESIDENT. You won't take me alive!

(**PRESIDENT** *charges, but Wham!* **ANNIE** *hits him in the head with a mannequin and he's knocked out.*)

ANNIE. You have no idea how much I've wanted to do that. I have a lot of anger inside me.

IFEZ. Thank goodness that's over.

ALIANA. There are three dead people in the closet.

IFEZ. ...Yeah. We made some poor choices. But we're continuing the show right?

ALIANA. One of the hosts is dead.

ANNIE. But did he really matter? I mean, you're the star of the show.

ALIANA. Thank you.

SHIVA. I've got an idea. We tie President up, put him in the closet, and then go to the runway.

ALIANA. That's crazy.

(Short pause.)

But that's what we do here on Project Design.

(Cheers from everyone.)

*(They drag **PRESIDENT** off.)*

*(**CAROL-ANN** steps forward.)*

CAROL-ANN. What did I say? Domination. Mic drop.

(Short pause.)

Can I get a mic? For the mic drop? Is there a way? Are we still rolling?

(Lights down.)

End of Play

(During the curtain call, it would be great if the actors could come out on the runway modeling their looks.)

ALTERNATE ENDING #5 (LUKE)

LUKE. Then who is it?

CAROL-ANN. Oh I think you know who it is, Jack.

LUKE. Jackson. I don't like nicknames.

CAROL-ANN. Ask me if I care if you don't like nicknames.

> *(Pause.)*

> I said ask me if I care.

LUKE. You actually want me to ask you?

CAROL-ANN. That's what I said.

LUKE. Okay. Do you care if –

CAROL-ANN. *(Cutting him off.)* I DO NOT! Because I know something about you – You're not a cop!

> *(Hushed gasps from everyone.)*

> You're actually...a fashion designer!

> *(Hushed gasps again.)*

LUKE. How dare you!

CAROL-ANN. You think the police department would send two undercover officers to the same show? You think they're that stupid? No I –

> *(Her cell phone rings.)*

> Hold on.

> Hello? Yeah, hi Chief. Oh. Okay.

> *(She hangs up.)*

> Okay, so you are an undercover cop. Fine, but that means you were in place before the death threat came in! You've been on the show since week one!

PRESIDENT. I've found most of his designs to be unimaginative, to tell you the truth.

IFEZ. Definitely.

LUKE. Yes I've been on this show since week one. Because this was never about murders. This was about getting deep undercover to expose...a bead smuggling ring!

IFEZ. What?

LUKE. That's right! We knew that one of you was smuggling illegal beads into the country from Canada and using them to decorate fanciful cat sweaters. There's only one way to put a stop to that. Spend forty thousand dollars on my undercover assignment. I went through intense training to get into the mind of a fashion designer, months of personal tutoring under Isaac Mizrahi, calisthenics to firm my buttocks –

CAROL-ANN. That explains it.

LUKE. All to bring down this bead smuggler.

PRESIDENT. It was Annie!

LUKE. Of course it was Annie!

ANNIE. Yeah, I import some beads from Canada.

LUKE. But you didn't declare them on your taxes!

ANNIE. Oh. Oh whoops.

LUKE. You owe seventeen dollars and ninety-five cents in back taxes!

ANNIE. Oh. Sorry.

LUKE. Scum like you makes me sick.

IFEZ. And I thought you were cool.

SHIVA. You did?

IFEZ. No I'm just saying that.

PRESIDENT. But if you were here to expose her bead-smuggling ring, then who's the killer?

CAROL-ANN. I'll answer that. Because I still know. Don't I, Jack-son?

LUKE. I don't know what you're talking about.

CAROL-ANN. You were here for Annie, but you got in too deep, didn't you? You figured out it was Annie right away, probably because you're not completely stupid.

ANNIE. Yeah I talked about my beads in the first episode.

CAROL-ANN. But you stayed. Why? Because you got a taste of fashion design. You got a taste of victory. It was like a drug to you, wasn't it? Sandra Bullock got to win, you wanted to win. And then you'd do anything to win, wouldn't you? Including...trying to kill all of your competitors! You tried to murder Ifez with the shears, you tried to kill Shiva with the needle, you were hoping to bash President over the head – but you forgot one thing... You suck at murder. Seriously. You are really terrible at it.

LUKE. I'm not so terrible that I can't kill you!

> (**LUKE** *charges* **CAROL-ANN**, *but Wham!* **ANNIE** *hits him on the back of the head with a mannequin, knocking him out.*)

ANNIE. Yeah you are.

IFEZ. Thank goodness that's over.

ALIANA. There are three dead people in the closet.

IFEZ. ...Yeah. We made some poor choices. But we're continuing the show right?

ALIANA. One of the hosts is dead.

ANNIE. But did he really matter? I mean, you're the star of the show.

ALIANA. Thank you.

SHIVA. I've got an idea. We tie Jackson up, put him in the closet, and then go to the runway.

ALIANA. That's crazy.

> (*Short pause.*)

But that's what we do here on Project Design.

> (*Cheers from everyone.*)
>
> (*They drag* **LUKE** *off.*)
>
> (**CAROL-ANN** *steps forward.*)

CAROL-ANN. What did I say? Domination. Mic drop.

> (*Short pause.*)

Can I get a mic? For the mic drop? Is there a way? Are we still rolling?

(Lights down.)

End of Play

(During the curtain call, it would be great if the actors could come out on the runway modeling their looks.)

ALTERNATE ENDING #6 (CAROL-ANN)

CAROL-ANN. But I think I know who it was.

ALIANA. Who?

CAROL-ANN. Society.

PRESIDENT. What?

CAROL-ANN. Think about it. Who's out there trying to bring us down? The Man.

IFEZ. Society didn't throw a pair of shears at my head.

CAROL-ANN. Didn't it?

IFEZ. No.

SHIVA. And society didn't stab me with a needle.

PRESIDENT. Or put a scorpion in the coffee.

LUKE. Or misspell the word "you're."

CAROL-ANN. Well it could've! Society can do all kinds of stuff you don't know about!

SHIVA. You are mentally disturbed.

CAROL-ANN. I'm a loose cannon!

PRESIDENT. Wait a minute, it was your sewing machine that got used.

SHIVA. And you have terrible grammar!

LUKE. And no one felt your butt to see if you were strong!

CAROL-ANN. I feel my own butt!

LUKE. She's the killer!

CAROL-ANN. I was sent here because someone on the show had threatened to murder someone live and –

ALIANA. Yeah that was us.

PRESIDENT. What?

ALIANA. We think it helps ratings. We make a few promos. But the producers didn't kill anyone. We just threaten every week.

LUKE. So it was you.

(Pause.)

(CAROL-ANN *grabs one of the mannequins.)*

CAROL-ANN. All right I admit it! I got in too deep! I thought I could just dip my toe into fashion design, but it's not something you can just sample! I loved it. Even though I couldn't use a sewing machine and I burned myself a lot! But still, the thrill of seeing your clothes come into creation...it was so intense, I had to win! I had to! And there was one problem! You were all better than me! So I had to kill you all to win!

ALIANA. I appreciate your spirit.

CAROL-ANN. Thank you! So...yes...I tried to kill you all! But I'm a better cop than a killer, and I couldn't –

> *(Wham!* **ANNIE** *hits* **CAROL-ANN** *on the back of the head with a mannequin.)*

ANNIE. Did anyone else hate her?

PRESIDENT. Yes. OMG.

IFEZ. I was gonna say something.

SHIVA. Well, I'm glad that's over with.

PRESIDENT. So what do we do now?

ALIANA. There are three dead people in the closet.

IFEZ. ...Yeah. We made some poor choices. But we're continuing the show right?

ALIANA. One of the hosts is dead.

ANNIE. But did he really matter? I mean, you're the star of the show.

ALIANA. Thank you.

SHIVA. I've got an idea. We tie her up, put her in the closet, and then go to the runway.

ALIANA. That's crazy.

> *(Short pause.)*

But that's what we do here on Project Design.

(Cheers from everyone.)
*(They drag **CAROL-ANN** off.)*
(Lights down.)

End of Play

(During the curtain call, it would be great if the actors could come out on the runway modeling their looks.)

ACTUAL ENDING #7 (ALIANA AND TOSCA)

> *(Feel free to use this ending if you like. You can also use this ending in addition to the audience-favorite. Whatever works for your production.)*

ALL. *(In the dark.)* But it actually happened like this!

> *(Lights back up – everyone is in the same position they were in before.)*

ALIANA. Then who is it?

CAROL-ANN. Oh I think you know the answer to that question. You were watching on camera, weren't you?

ALIANA. We try not to watch. It's too sad.

CAROL-ANN. But you were watching this time. And recording.

ALIANA. I don't know what you're talking about.

CAROL-ANN. Don't you? What kind of show would keep filming when one of its stars was killed?

PRESIDENT. Reality show?

CAROL-ANN. Yes, okay –

SHIVA. Pretty sure the Bravo network would do it –

CAROL-ANN. All right, good point.

LUKE. TLC would do it.

CAROL-ANN. Okay, fine, most networks would keep filming. But keeping us trapped in here, while murders were continuing? Who stands to benefit from that? The network!

> *(She points at **ALIANA**.)*

Why did they send a recorded message to the police department? Why did they allow me and Luke to go undercover? Why did they keep turning out the lights? Because they were the ones doing the killing!

> *(Everyone seems convinced by this.)*

SHIVA. That's the first time you've actually made logical sense.

ALIANA. Designers...please...this woman is a lunatic.

ANNIE. That's true. But she seems to have a point.

PRESIDENT. I hate to admit it, but she's making sense.

CAROL-ANN. None of these people here have the butt-strength to throw a pair of shears into a wall! Only one person on this show could do that!

ALIANA. You certainly can't mean me.

CAROL-ANN. I don't. I mean...

(She points dramatically.)

HIM!

*(**TOSCA** enters.)*

TOSCA. Good morning designers.

IFEZ. AAAAAH!

PRESIDENT. You're alive?! But the person here with no medical training thought you were dead!

CAROL-ANN. That's actually my bad.

TOSCA. Child's play. I'm very relaxed. I can slow my breathing to the point where someone wouldn't be able to detect it.

ANNIE. Wow.

TOSCA. And then you put me in the closet.

PRESIDENT. So sorry about that.

TOSCA. It's fine. You were doing what I wanted. Making it work.

PRESIDENT. Is that what you mean by that? Even if you're killed, to keep going?

TOSCA. Essentially.

CAROL-ANN. I began to suspect it wasn't one of us when Shiva found the scorpion in the coffee. Nobody here is man enough to handle a scorpion.

LUKE. True.

IFEZ. I find them icky.

SHIVA. I could do it.

CAROL-ANN. Yes, but you were the one who found it. Then, there was the issue of the poisoned hot glue.

IFEZ. Who did that?

CAROL-ANN. Nobody. The producers just skimped on materials and got some substandard hot glue.

PRESIDENT. I knew it! Well you're liable for a lawsuit now, lady!

ALIANA. Actually, when you signed your waiver, you agreed not to hold us liable.

PRESIDENT. Darn!

CAROL-ANN. Which brings us to that other girl. What's-her-name?

SHIVA. Which one?

CAROL-ANN. The other model. The second one who died.

PRESIDENT. I tried not to learn their names.

CAROL-ANN. The one who got bludgeoned. It'll come to me tonight when I'm going to sleep.

IFEZ. Who cares what her name was, how did she get killed?

CAROL-ANN. Running with scissors.

PRESIDENT. No!

CAROL-ANN. Yep! I noticed the scissors in her hands at the time of death. She ran around with them – and died instantly. Never run with scissors.

SHIVA. So it was an accident?

CAROL-ANN. Indeed.

SHIVA. So there were no murders at all?

ALIANA. Nope.

SHIVA. Then who stabbed me with a needle?

(**ANNIE** *raises her hand.*)

ANNIE. I did. I have a lot of rage. I was trying to kill you.

CAROL-ANN. Trying. She was trying. But she didn't succeed. No harm, no foul.

SHIVA. I got stabbed. That's harm!

CAROL-ANN. Only a little bit. But it's not a crime to try to kill someone, it's only a crime to succeed.

SHIVA. It's *attempted* murder!

CAROL-ANN. Get over yourself. Seriously.

PRESIDENT. But why did you do all of this?

ALIANA. Isn't it obvious? Ratings.

TOSCA. It will be phenomenal. So...designers...you have five minutes to get your looks ready...make sure to make liberal use of the accessory wall, and meet us on the runway. One of you will be named the winner...and one of you...will be eliminated.

ALIANA. See you on the runway!

> *(They exit.)*
>
> *(Pause.)*

CAROL-ANN. Well, I'm glad that turned out well.

> (**SHIVA** *stares at* **ANNIE.**)

SHIVA. I'm going to kill you.

ANNIE. Not if I kill you first.

> *(Everyone grabs their clothes and starts getting ready –)*
>
> *(Lights out.)*
>
> *(Scream!)*

End of Play

> *(During the curtain call, it would be great if the actors could come out on the runway modeling their looks.)*